Kingsholt

Kingsholt

Susan Holliday

OUR STREET
BOOKS

Winchester, UK
Washington, USA

First published by Our Street Books, 2015
Our Street Books is an imprint of John Hunt Publishing Ltd., Laurel House, Station Approach,
Alresford, Hants, SO24 9JH, UK
office1@jhpbooks.net
www.johnhuntpublishing.com
www.ourstreet-books.com

For distributor details and how to order please visit the 'Ordering' section on our website.

Text copyright: Susan Holliday 2014

ISBN: 978 1 78279 976 4
Library of Congress Control Number: 2014956730

A CIP catalogue record for this book is available from the British Library.

Design: Stuart Davies

Printed and bound by CPI Group (UK) Ltd, Croydon, CR0 4YY, UK

We operate a distinctive and ethical publishing philosophy in all
areas of our business, from our global network of authors to
production and worldwide distribution.

For Jess with love

Prologue

...the Vikings were a frightening sight in their pointed helmets and fierce armour. They threw burning straw into the wooden outbuildings, pulled down the living quarters and stripped the church of its treasures. They slaughtered the monks and feasted in the midst of the carnage. They left at dusk, throwing burning torches into the fields and shouting their songs of victory. The next day the few monks who escaped crept back from the woods to bury the dead. They dug a pit and placed their bodies in the mass grave. Some were clothed in their blood stained rough woollen garments, others were naked. They said prayers and threw earth over their bodies. They forbad anyone to open up the pit...

from The Chronicle of Kingsholt 1890

Chapter One

Sam dribbled the football down the narrow corridor and towards the envelope that lay askew on the front door mat. As he picked up the letter his heart beat faster than he liked to admit. It was Chloe's writing all right, but more ragged than it used to be, as if she'd gone backwards since she was twelve. *Something has happened,* he thought.

He looked inside and drew out two pieces of paper torn from an old exercise book. Was his cousin plunged into dire poverty or something? Or was she just not bothering? He unfolded the letter slowly, half afraid of what he would read.

Kingsholt Monks Lane, Devon
Dear Sam,
Sorry I haven't replied for ages and sorry I missed your thirteenth birthday. I hope we're still speaking! Wait for the long whinge! I simply don't like being here. Can't put my finger on it but that's how it is. Funny feelings.

Sam pulled a face. What did she mean, *funny feelings?*
He went back to the letter.

First there's my new school. The kids hate me because I haven't got a Devon accent and because I've inherited a mansion, even if it's crumbling. There's one girl who's a right bully and the others copy – you know how it is.

At home things aren't much better. As you know it's nearly two years since Uncle George was found dead in the woods and Dad and Mum are still trying to work it out. Mum's vague as usual and spends half her time doing up our old house for letting, while a nice lady called Leela helps out here. She has a son called Tyler, about twelve, like me, but he's really big and strong. He has a dog and a cow, of all things and I think he's a bit strange. *Dad's never around – we're just that much too far out for him to get to work easily, so he often stays away in the company flat. That leaves Aidan to look after everything.* He first met Uncle George on a retreat at Lindisfarne or something. *Uncle George asked him to help turn Kingsholt into a sort of Christian Centre for no-go kids. Some chance!*

(Three days later)

Sorry about the gap. I've been in what you might call nowhere land. Can't explain it really. Anyway, back to my letter. Where was I? That's right! Aidan. I think he's a bit of a dark horse and for some reason he's crazy about King Alfred. You know, the one who burned the cakes. He spends hours and hours in the library and when he comes out he looks really remote, as if he's living in another world. He's talking about building a chapel in the wood or something but he must be crazy – there's no money about at all.

It's like being in the Dark Ages. Nothing works and animals are all over the place. There's sheep, goats and a bird hospital that was started by Uncle George. Tell you more when I see you. Love to Auntie Jane.

Love, Chloe.

Sam folded up the letter and put it back into the envelope.

It's 1985, he thought, and my cousin says she's in the Dark Ages. It's unbelievable.

He walked over to the window. All right, Cheriton Street, Balham wasn't the most inspiring place and their house was pretty small, but wasn't it better to spend the summer here, than in a crumbling mansion in the middle of nowhere? Besides, this wasn't the Chloe he used to know. She'd always been cheerful and he'd even once, fool that he was, written a poem about her. He must have been out of his mind. Anyway that was ages ago.

Maybe he should show the letter to Mum. She was the only one around who knew Chloe as well as he did. Perhaps she might understand what was going on.

At six-thirty, his mother came swinging through the door calling, 'Hi, Sam! Here I am!' It was her cheery way of saying, I'm sorry I'm later than ever.

She rushed into the small, warm kitchen, pink from hurrying, and dumped her shopping bag on the table. Sam towered over her, pulling a face, and she smiled.

'You've definitely grown today, Sam. You're a tall one for thirteen. And you're not the only one. The girls at school are like Amazons!'

She scrabbled into her shopping bag. 'Fish and chips tonight. They say fish is good for your brains!'

She shared out the meal on two plain white plates. 'I forgot to tell you, I was helping with the church garden after school. You've no idea how quickly the weeds move in.'

The meal was rapidly restoring Sam's natural good nature. 'Talking of moving in,' he said, dashing vinegar over his battered cod, 'I had this letter from Chloe. Months of silence and then *this*.'

Mum put on her gold rimmed glasses. 'Well, at least you've got a letter.'

She read it carefully. 'Odd,' she said. 'But it's none of my business, none at all. It really is up to Dorothy and Jack to do something about the whole set-up. They wouldn't thank me for interfering. Especially as I've hardly heard from them since Uncle George's funeral. Mind you, writing was never their priority.' She shook her head. 'Do you remember what lovely times we used to have by the sea?'

Sam had a vision of green-blue waves and sand and Chloe running along the beach with the sun shining on her thin, brown body, her long fair hair lifting in the wind.

They finished their meal in thoughtful silence, then Sam clattered the plates together and stacked them in the sink. That's how they always worked since Dad had walked out, four years ago: one day he washed up and Mum cooked, the next day he cooked and Mum washed up. And sometimes, like today, she brought in fish and chips because it was getting late and she was tired.

'Ice-cream for seconds,' she said, bringing out a carton from the fridge and cutting off two large slices.

'I don't know if I want to go to Kingsholt in the summer,' said Sam, 'I don't like the sound of it.'

'Don't give up on it yet,' said Mum. 'It's a beautiful place, or was on the day of poor Uncle George's funeral. One of those lovely November days when it still feels like summer.'

'Was it?' he asked. That was when he was in bed with flu, and had this vision of Dad in green pyjamas at the bottom of his bed. Or thought he had.

'I have an old postcard of the mansion somewhere.'

His mother scrabbled in a drawer. 'Here we are. *And* some writing on the back.' She put on her glasses again.

'Kingsholt is a tall, early Victorian mansion made from local stone, set in a green valley and surrounded by woods and hills. Long ago its hunt balls were famous, its front drive resounded with the life and colour of dogs and horses and brightly dressed huntsmen.'

She looked up and laughed. 'Not a very politically correct postcard but historically true. I remember seeing a print hanging in the hall. There was your father's great-grandfather holding the reins of a handsome Irish Hunter and in the background, dogs and huntsmen crowding together before the porch.'

'I don't know what Chloe's groaning about,' he muttered. 'It sounds good to me. That doesn't mean I want to go, of course.'

His mother put away the postcard. 'After the exams you can sort out what you want to do in the summer. For the moment it's worth putting all you have into your work.'

'Come off it, Mum, you're not at school now.'

Mum smiled. 'You'll be pleased to hear, I'm not just a teacher but a slave as well. Listen to this. I've decided to take on *all* domestic duties, so you can settle down to your end of term revision. You didn't do so well last term, did you?'

'But I like cooking,' Sam teased, 'and anyway, the exams aren't important.'

He wandered up to his room and read the letter again. Why should he reply yet when Chloe had taken so long to get her fingers round a biro? He put the letter away in his table drawer and opened his maths book. But he couldn't concentrate, so he took out his pens and ink and practised his calligraphy. There were only two of them doing it and he didn't want to let the teacher down. Besides, he enjoyed writing, it soothed him and he was naturally good at it.

He wrote: *Dear Chloe, I hate you, I'm not going to have anything more to do with you.* Then he tore it up and took out the calligraphy exam question: *Make a map of Treasure Island to the following scale.*

He had already finished planning the project. He would write in his best italic hand and decorate the map with little drawings of Long John Silver and barrels of rum and a parrot. He would write the title in Roman Capitals.

It was no good. He took Chloe's letter out of the drawer and read it again. Perhaps it wasn't her fault she'd turned into a whingey twelve-year-old. But he wouldn't write back, he thought, not until after the exams. Not because of Mum but because he wouldn't. And he was not going down there in the summer, that was for sure.

Three weeks later, on a sun-filled Saturday morning, another letter came, or rather, a note. The writing was just as bad, as if Chloe was getting at him for liking calligraphy. When Mum brought it to his room with a slavish bow, he was putting the finishing touches to his map of Treasure Island. When he had carefully washed his pens (Dad had always said you have to look after your tools) he slumped down on his bed and held Chloe's cheap, lined paper in his inky hands.

He read carefully

Dear Sam,

Perhaps my other letter didn't get to you. Or maybe you've given me up. Weird things are happening and I do want you to come in the summer. I have a friend here and he's told me something unbelievable. He says, two years ago, Uncle George killed his daughter, Rosie. He has put up a memorial to her in the wood.
Can we fix the date?
Love Chloe.

Sam swung his legs over the side of the narrow bed and sat there. The letter filled him with a dark foreboding – the sort of feeling he had had when Mum picked up the note his father had left on the mantlepiece, underneath the clock. First Dad walking out then Chloe going off her head! It was too much!

'Air,' he thought and walked out.

He strode up the hill to the common and immediately felt different. Perhaps Chloe should come here instead. But it wasn't on. There wasn't enough room. He hurried over the common, hoping to come across the gang. But no one was about and his conscience was pricked. They must be revising. It was only two days to the first history paper. Good job he had a photographic memory.

He circled round and came out on the road again, taking the longer route home. It led him past Mum's church and the little garden she looked after. He went through the gate and up the path that led to the porch. To his surprise, the oak door to the church was half open. Someone must be about. He hadn't sung in the choir since he was ten and he'd given up church when he got into the football team. But he always felt at home in this red brick, Victorian building. He walked up the side aisle, to where the white candles were burning and put a10p piece in the little wooden chest. He carefully lit a candle from another and pressed it down over one of the iron spikes. He hadn't done this for months, not since he came to the conclusion that a candle would never show Dad the way home. He couldn't explain why he was moved to do it now. There was no knowing. Or maybe it was because, at that moment, there didn't seem to be anyone else around who would light one for Chloe.

Chapter Two

He's right, thought Chloe. Aidan's right! There's a darkness in this valley. It's bad enough at school with all the bullying but here —

She leaned against the gate at the top of the long, winding drive and stared down at Kingsholt. She could hardly believe it was hers, or to be more accurate, theirs, – though Mum and Dad were so often away, it seemed as if the big old house only belonged to her.

What has happened, she wondered, for everything to have grown so lonely and neglected, deprived of its old happiness? Even from this distance, she could see how dilapidated the building had become. Tiles were slipping off the roof and one tall chimney sloped dangerously as if it had been pushed over by a gust of wind. The stone lintels were covered in creeping ivy; the windows were grey and dusty, so you couldn't see through them. The pillars under the front porch leaned outwards, as if they were about to collapse, and on one side of the drive a stone saluki dog leaned forward, one leg bent, his feathery tail held high. Chloe imagined there was a taut, strained look to his head, as if he was listening, despite his broken ear, to all the dark rumours that she herself had half-heard.

Everything's gone wrong, she thought, ever since Uncle George was found dead. For once her father had been around to discuss it.

'My brother wasn't old or ill,' he had said, with an unusually bleak gaze. 'Everyone respected him for all his 'rescue' work. We even call him, St George, don't we? Or did.'

Chloe had known Dad was speaking in a chopped up way so he wouldn't show his feelings too much. His blue eyes had looked pale and watery.

'He was good to everyone,' he went on. 'Aidan says as much

and if anyone's reliable he is.' He spoke more sharply. 'Aidan has his own thoughts about our brother's death and so have I.'

From that moment rumours grew like creeping ivy.

Chloe stared for a long time at the big house in the valley. Aidan told her there had once been a monastery here and a stone mine that went right back to the Romans. Somewhere, he said, there were underground passages, but no one knew where.

She imagined the valley had not changed very much since old times; the fields and trees and the little stream that ran by the house were full of echoes of the past.

She looked round. The wood where Aidan had found Uncle George was on her left, across a field where a few sheep were grazing. She had avoided going there before but now she somehow wanted to find the place where his body had been found. She stepped off the gate and went through a trail of sunshine and grass, to the edge of the tall pines. As she went deeper into the wood, the trees closed in on her and the air grew thicker and hotter. She could smell something rotten and stopped where the path was blocked by a branch.

Just in front of her was a tree that had been struck by lightning. A few dead leaves clung to its twisted branches, like shrivelled creatures that could not let go. A short inscription was incised in the stripped trunk, so low down it was half hidden by undergrowth. She pushed the brambles aside and stared at the letters:

ROSIE, UNFORGOTTEN.

She remembered what Aidan had once told her when she came with Mum and Dad to look over Kingsholt.

'It's my belief this area is under a curse. It must be or George would never have been killed.'

Maybe Rosie was killed as well.

A deep voice echoed her thoughts. 'Summat dreadful

happened here!'

Chloe jumped and turned round. A little way off in the under-growth a man stood, watching her. He was tall, with black hair tied in a rough ponytail and dark eyes that softened as he examined Chloe. 'Twelve, is it?'

'How do you know?' Chloe bit her lip. Why on earth did she allow herself to reply to a stranger?

'Our Rosie was twelve when George Penfold killed her.'

'Whatever do you mean?' she asked, torn between outrage and curiosity and a desire to run away.

'I won't harm you,' he said softly, answering her thoughts.

Chloe walked quickly down the path.

'Nimbus,' he shouted after her, 'that's who I am.'

But Chloe was thinking of her cousin Sam. She felt guilty because she hadn't written to him for months and now suddenly she longed for him to be with her. Not that Nimbus had done anything wrong. It was just his intense look that frightened her and the way he stared at the bony branches of the tree, as if they pointed to a truth no one else could understand.

She broke into a run. The same thought kept going through her head: if Uncle George *really* killed Rosie, how could she believe *anything* again? He had been her kindly uncle, bringing her pocket money or sweets. 'The daughter I never had,' he had once said.

Later that evening, when they were eating in the kitchen, Chloe told her mother how she had met Nimbus and what he had said. Mum dismissed the accusation with a laugh. 'Of course Uncle George didn't kill Rosie. It was an accident. She ran out when he was felling the tree. It's grief speaking, my dear. No parent can get over the death of a child.'

Aidan leaned towards Chloe. 'Keep away from Nimbus,' he said in his deep, even voice. 'He's a bitter man, especially these days. He has a new partner but it hasn't worked out. As you're beginning to understand, there's more to Kingsholt than meets the eye. Terrible things once happened in this valley and history always has its echoes. It's those echoes we must fight if we are ever going to bring peace to this place again. Mind you, there are good corners. The little cottage where Leela and Tyler live has always been untouched by any darkness and let's pray Leela will keep it that way.'

Chloe left her omelette piled on one side of her dish. She slipped through the kitchen door and ran up two floors to her room. Lying on the bed, she looked up at the torn wall paper. Small bits flapped from the ceiling like brown moths. Sunlight smeared the dusty window that overlooked the valley and hills at the front of the house. If she did up her bedroom she would feel better. Or would she? Perhaps she should write to Sam again, at least he lived in a normal world. She looked round for a biro and scraps of paper and scrawled hurriedly. But she hadn't written to him for ages and it wasn't good enough so she screwed up the letter and threw it on the floor. She would try again later.

Still feeling unsettled, she ran downstairs, found some stale bread in the kitchen and went up to the hospital cage where Aidan looked after the wounded animals and birds.

'At least everyone can see what's the matter with you,' she told them, stuffing the bread through the wire. A rook hopped over to grab the largest crust and she was so absorbed watching the scared smaller birds peck and run, that she was unaware of anyone approaching.

'There's many a bird with a broken wing,' said a voice behind her. Chloe jumped and wheeled round to face Nimbus.

'What are *you* doing here?'

'Walking. I often walk in the evening. '

'I haven't seen you round here before,' she said.

Nimbus nodded. 'I've kept myself to myself but from now on things are going to be different.'

He stared at the cage. 'I'm glad you've come,' he said. 'My Rosie liked animals like you. She had a barrel laid on its side

12

where she kept ferrets.She watched them for hours in their run.'

He was holding a child's plastic bucket full of worms and he threw them through the cage bars. The birds vied with each other to peck at them.

'Survival of the fittest,' he said, nodding at a blackbird with a trailing wing. *'He* won't make it, not for long.'

After that Chloe often met Nimbus wandering about the valley. He would show her the wild flowers, the birds, the badger holes and the secret tracks where the foxes walked. And yet there was no subject that did not lead him back to Rosie. Perhaps it was because of her own unsettled feelings that she found herself becoming more trusting.

She was off her guard when he first offered her the pills. It was the day when the bully at school had shown up her accent by mimicking her and making the others laugh.

'This'll help,' he said when she told him – and it was true.

That afternoon her spirits lifted, she felt as if even school would never get her down again. From then on, whenever she was depressed, she took what he offered and liked the way he included her, as if he was her ally against her new school and this great ruin of a house and all the grandiose plans. Yet she didn't altogether trust him. As the days passed, she realized there was something strange and bitter about the way he talked to her, almost as if – dare she think it – as if it was all her fault that Rosie had died. But then his voice would turn soft and lingering, so she couldn't resist it. He had a deep, commanding voice, not like Dad, who often sounded breathless and exhausted, or Mum, who was always sighing. Chloe found herself telling him about her old house and the friends she really missed. But she never mentioned Sam. There was no need, she thought.

Chapter Three

One day Nimbus said to Chloe, 'Come up to my place. You can meet Gina and the baby, and maybe you can help Tammy. She can't read any more than I can.'

Chloe toyed with the idea for a long time, peeping from her bedroom window at the stone cottage on the slope above the wood. Then, one Saturday, when no one else was about, she found herself walking towards it, holding a book for Tammy, as if someone else had decided for her. She had refused to accompany Mum and Dad to the market, watching them sweep up the drive in the Range Rover, stopping while Mum opened the gate. Her mother had turned and waved, and for a moment, Chloe wished she had gone with them. Then the car disappeared round the corner and she caught sight of the smoke rising from Nimbus's cottage like a signal.

She went quickly through the dark wood, past the dead tree – the Nimbus Tree – and out onto the sloping field where the stone building stood. It was dilapidated, with a lopsided front door and a garden overgrown with thistles. Rusty toys lay about in the grass and Nimbus was holding an axe in both hands, swinging the blade down onto a large log.

'Mind the thistles,' he said but it was too late. Chloe tripped over a stone and put out her hand to keep her balance. A small prick of blood rose on her forefinger, a tiny, bright red sphere.

Wiping it away, she looked up. A little way off, a girl – surely it was Tammy – was sitting on the grass, painting her toe nails bright red.

'I've brought you a book,' said Chloe, ' We could read it together.'

'No point.' Tammy, barely looking up, 'I've finished school.'

'How old are you then?'

'Sixteen, aren't I?'

She was slight boned with a mass of auburn hair round her pale face and blank eyes, one hazel, one green. She's more like twelve, thought Chloe, and it's not just her looks. It's the way she's painting her toenails, hunched up, intense, private, like a twelve year old acting big. She doesn't like me, she thought.

'Your dad wants you to learn to read,' she said, 'and I've especially chosen this book. It's about a girl who hears voices. Well, it's about St. Joan —'

Tammy laughed. 'Hears voices? I do that all right, don't I Dad?'

Nimbus put down his axe and looked up. His brown arms glistened with sweat. His jeans were torn at the knee and his old vest was full of holes.

Tammy screwed the lid onto the bottle of nail varnish, took the book from Chloe and hurled it at the house. 'That's what I think of that.'

'It's not mine,' said Chloe angrily. 'It's from Kingsholt. And if you feel like that I won't bother again.' She ran to pick it up. To her surprise Nimbus threw back his brown head and laughed.

'She's like me, eh? No truck with reading or writing. Give it a miss today, Chloe. Who knows, Tammy might end up carrying everything up here, see?' He tapped his head. 'Can you read my mind, Tammy?'

'Sometimes,' said Tammy, shooting him a conspiratorial look.

She went indoors while Nimbus picked up his axe again and felt its edge. His arm swung back and down and the log sprang apart. He spoke softly as if he knew what Chloe was feeling. 'There'll be other days. She'll get by, people like us always do. Come on in and eat with us, Chloe. We got baked taters today. She's good at baked taters is our Tammy.'

Dark and dusty, thought Chloe as she stepped inside the cottage. An old-fashioned iron stove stood inside the wide chimney place. It had two doors side by side, one for the oven, the other for the fire. Wood ash filtered down onto the stone floor and over the rag rug that spread, discoloured and dull, before the hearth. Tammy knelt down, opened the door of the oven and poked at the jacket potatoes with a sharp knife.

She'll never be my friend, thought Chloe.

Nimbus took off his boots and stretched out on a ragged couch that was covered with a dirty tartan rug. 'Got some for *her* then?'

'Plenty of jackets,' said Tammy. 'They're good and ready.' She grinned and waved the knife at Chloe. 'We don't use these things, see? We use these.' She held up her small red-nailed hands.

'Fingers and newspaper,' said Nimbus. 'That's when you really taste the food. Like taters?'

Chloe nodded.

'Gina and the baby won't be back from the market yet. We might as well begin.'

Tammy took hold of a dirty cloth and pulled an iron tray out of the small oven. They all sat on the floor and held the potatoes in napkins of newspaper. It's a *truthful* way of life, thought Chloe, not bothering about knives and forks. No thick butter or creamy milk, just potatoes and a glass of water.

They ate in silence, until Nimbus wiped his mouth with the back of his hand and spoke in a slow voice. 'So you've inherited Kingsholt, is that right?'

'My Dad has. I don't want it, I never did. It's big and ugly.'

Nimbus crashed his free fist onto the ground. 'It's a palace,' he said fiercely, 'and by any rights it should be ours. Your Uncle George killed our Rosie and left us nothing. We have nothing. NOTHING. *I* can't work now I'm not in the circus.'

Chloe had never seen his eyes flash like that, black, angry eyes.

'He used to be a hypnotist and a trapeze artiste,' said Tammy, nodding at her father. 'That was before he hurt his foot.' She looked up proudly. 'I've seen him walk the sky. Until he fell.'

Chloe whistled. It was all Dad could do to crawl into the car.

She peered down at Nimbus's feet, then at one of the big dusty boots lined with newspaper.

'I was lucky not to be dead,' he said. Then, after a while, 'Enjoying it?'

Chloe nodded and wiped her mouth with her hand as he had done.

Nimbus finished eating, screwed up the newspaper into a ball and threw it into the stove. A fierce orange flame shot up.

'Tammy would like you around, wouldn't you, Tammy? Reading or no reading.'

'Instead of Rosie?' asked Tammy, both eyes blank.

Nimbus ignored her and smiled at Chloe. 'When you come up here I'll teach you —' He broke off and brought more logs for the fire.

'We keep it going all the year round,' he said, shoving on another log and carelessly raking the ash, 'no matter how hot it be. This is a cold cottage at the best of times.' He looked intently at Chloe. 'It's in the stones, my dear, and in the history.'

'How do you mean?' said Chloe.

Chapter Four

It was two weeks later when Nimbus told Chloe all about the cottage. She had often met him in the valley but had never gone back to the pest house on the hill. There was something about it that made her afraid.

'Come on up,' said Nimbus on a day when she was feeling very isolated. 'Tammy's wondering why she never sees you. She gets out of sorts, does our Tammy, without her sister or her mother.' Loneliness was something Chloe understood, so this time she went up to the cottage and Nimbus took her inside. No one else was in the room.

'It's called the pest house,' he said, 'and that's what it was.' He pointed to the rough wall on the right of the window. 'In the very old part over there – that's where them with the plague were left to die.'

Chloe looked at the dark corner of the room. Shadows and cobwebs flapped from the ceiling, and on the flint wall a corn dolly, a horseshoe and a black pendant hung from three rusty nails. Nimbus's words came out oddly, as if he was using someone else's voice.

'Aye, the Black Death. Blood spitting, putrid inflammation, black spots, tumours on thighs and arms.'

Tammy clattered downstairs and smirked as if she had been listening. Chloe's mind raced back to the lesson in school about the fourteenth century, when the Black Death had killed over a third of the population of England. She touched the walls and imagined she heard the ring of the death bell and a voice calling, 'Throw out your dead, throw out your dead.' She rubbed her eyes. Dad always said she had too much imagination for her own good.

Nimbus took the pendant from the wall. It was jet black and shiny and there was a hole in the top where a thin thread of leather had been strung. A funny sort of thing to have, thought Chloe as he swung it in front of her. She found herself looking at it intently, backwards and forwards, backwards and forwards.

'Backwards and forwards,' Nimbus was saying in a soft hypnotic voice, 'backwards and forwards, like the buzzard that flies free in the wood.' He paused. 'There are secrets, Chloe, grave matters to resolve, things to find out. You must do as we do, think as we think. Be one of us, one of the Nimbus tribe. And never listen to Aidan. He has nothing to tell you but lies. Come now, look into my eyes —'

Chloe met his gaze and found herself leaning towards Nimbus, as if he was a magnet. It was like the dream she sometimes had, when she couldn't move, although a great black rock was about to tumble on her. Yet always, at the last minute, she stepped aside and the rock fell a little way off without harming her. He began to count slowly down from ten and Chloe found herself swaying to his voice as if it was quite a natural thing to do. The pendant traced smaller and smaller arcs and eventually came to a standstill. Nimbus was silent for a while and then he spoke. Although Chloe could never recall what he said, she remembered the bitter conviction in his voice.

With an enormous effort she moved away from him. A little later she had an uneasy feeling something strange had happened. She looked round but nothing very much had changed. Only Tammy had moved and was stuffing tight balls of newspaper into the fire, her red hair glowing in the colour of the shooting flames.

'I must go now,' said Chloe hurriedly. 'I've got things to do.'

Nimbus hung the pendant back over the rusty nail. 'Children are always in a hurry. But I'm not. I have time. Plenty of time.' He saw her to the door. 'You will come back, won't you? I've a thing or two to sort out and I could do with your help.'

Chloe nodded and went out into the sunshine. She walked quickly down through the wood, fearful that Nimbus would come after her, yet wondering why she was so afraid. He and Tammy were her friends, weren't they, needing her help, asking her to go back? Of course, Mum had told her not to talk to strangers but he wasn't a stranger, was he? He was part of Kingsholt.

There was a sudden ruffle in the trees overhead and through the shadows she saw a buzzard land high up in a tree, neck forward, wings back, ready to swoop. She froze, as an animal might, until the buzzard beat upwards again and left behind nothing but a few falling leaves. That was when she became aware of a strange putrid smell and a whining sound that might be Aidan's saw.

He's probably spying while he's up in the tree, she thought and stopped dead in her tracks. What had made her think that? How had that thought come into her head? In a moment of panic she broke into a run, taking a short cut through the undergrowth so that she would avoid the Nimbus Tree.

Beyond the wood the sun lay in great sheaves over the fields, and at the bottom of the valley, the little stream shone like silver paper. Chloe watched the brown meadow butterflies flit over the grass. Ewes were grazing with their half-grown lambs under the chestnut tree. Slowly her feelings of unease and fear drained away. It was as if they belonged to another life she had left behind, on the other side of the wood. She decided to leave it behind forever.

'Now this should tempt you,' said Mrs Penfold, as Chloe walked into the kitchen. The table was piled high with fruit – apples and oranges, bananas and melons.

'Enough to feed an army!' Dorothy Penfold said, peering at her daughter carefully. 'You're looking peaky, darling. Well, here's something to cheer you up.'

'I'm all right, really I am,' Chloe told her as she took the letter her mother was holding out and opened it.

Cheriton rd. Balham. July 4th .

Dear Chloe,
In a fortnight Mum's off to Lindisfarne with her friend (following Uncle George's footsteps) so I thought I'd come down, even though you seem to be wrapped up with this weirdo and his daughter. Or, to be nearer the truth, my mother, who doesn't teach Amazons for nothing, pressed me to come and see you. She's a tiny tyrant who rules me with a rod of iron and in the end I said yes.
p.s. I'll come back if it doesn't work out.
Cheers, Sam

Chloe handed the letter to her mother and leaned out of the window, secretly pleased. Sam would make everything normal again, just as it used to be. Aidan was in the yard feeding the chickens and from behind, her mother's voice filled the kitchen with waves of comment and information. '…Trust Dad to ask me to be with him just the week that Sam's coming. I'll just have time to settle him down, then I'll be off to some retirement do in London, then back to the other house, and up to London again. It's unremitting, isn't it darling? And of course I won't go if you're still under the weather.'

'I'll be fine, Mum,' said Chloe without turning round.

The voice went on, bouncing off different corners of the kitchen. 'Leela will be here to keep an eye on you all. Mind you, she'll have to go back in the evening to feed Tyler but I know she'll sleep over if need be. Such a kind person, and of course Aidan is a gem.'

Chloe turned round and watched her mother sit down at the table, her chin cupped in her hands. 'It all seems rather difficult doesn't it, darling? I sometimes wish we could go back in time.'

'That's a thought,' said Chloe. 'I'd go back any day.'

Her mother uttered a little sigh. 'It's too late, pet. You know Dad's had enough of London. He really does want to develop this place and spend more time with us at the same time. And he will one day. It's the best way through, I'm sure of that. Besides, Uncle George wouldn't want us to abandon the ship.'

'Dad always says he wants to be with us,' said Chloe, 'but he never is. I don't remember the last time I went for a walk with him. I reckon he couldn't walk properly if he tried.'

Her mother shrugged her shoulders and looked dreamily out of the window. 'By the way, Chloe, have you seen Aidan wearing his tree climbing gear. Talk about old fashioned. But he seems determined to let in the light and make a clearing for the chapel he and Uncle George planned.'

Chloe spoke quickly. 'He's always creeping around in those woods as if he's on to something. I shouldn't trust him if I were you.'

'Whatever do you mean, pet?'

Chloe watched her mother's face sag into anxiety. 'I don't believe in the chapel idea for a moment. Where's the money coming from? He's crazy.'

Her mother sighed. 'He's a good man, Chloe, honest as the day is long. It's simply that Uncle George had a mission, and he wants to fulfil it. Besides, I really couldn't do without him. For instance, tonight, he's promised to cook for you while I'm at the concert. Didn't I tell you?'

'You're always doing something,' said Chloe taking back Sam's letter and reading it again.

That evening, Aidan cooked two trout he had caught in the stream.

'We should have a trout farm,' he said. 'We might make some money that way.'

'It's delicious,' said Chloe, squeezing half a lemon onto the crisp, shiny trout skin. 'Just what I like to eat. I had a meal at Nimbus's cottage the other day —'

'So you've been —?'

She spoke sharply, 'What's wrong?'

Aidan stopped picking at the fine bones of the fish. 'It's hard to explain, Chloe, let alone believe. Things have become overshadowed in the valley. '

'It's all rubbish!' she said, but she didn't mean it. They ate in silence, then she stood up and collected the plates and handed Aidan the fruit bowl. He picked off a few grapes and she took a small red apple and held it up.

'I loved being in our other house,' she told him, 'but I have a funny feeling about this whole valley.' She became silent again then looked straight at Aidan.

'I wish I could go away.'

She bit the apple and looked round. 'How did this place get like this?'

'Money,' said Aidan flatly. 'Your Uncle George ran out of money. He was always helping people of course, but he wasn't very practical. Nor was his father or grandfather. This place was in a pretty bad way when *he* took it on.' He looked up quickly. 'And yet once upon a time there was nothing but happiness here. It'll come back one day. Listen Chloe, I've discovered something.'

But she wasn't listening. All she could hear was the slamming of a door inside her head, the turning of a key. 'I don't want to hear it,' she said, a break in her voice. She hurled the rest of the apple at the wall and stamped to the door. 'I don't trust you, Aidan. I don't know why, but I don't trust anyone anymore.'

Chapter Five

Sam stood up and looked out of his bedroom window. Whatever am I doing here, he thought?

The sun was turning red and leaden, slinking into clouds that looked like those dusty plush cushions in the living room. This place was spooky all right, and had been from the moment Aunt Dorothy had met him at the station without Chloe. 'Sorry dear, she's exploring the grounds,' was all the explanation she had offered as they drove into the Devon countryside. It was bad enough without Chloe, but as the lanes became narrower and the hedges higher, he had felt enclosed, even captured. Would he ever get back to Cheriton Street, Balham? His feelings intensified when they turned into a lane edged with high banks and overhung with thick, old trees.

'There's an iron age fort up there. It's called Blackburr Fort.'

His aunt had slowed up and pointed to the right where high banks encircled a flat area of open grass, broken up by a few tall trees. It was at that moment Sam thought he had seen someone peering out behind a branch, smiling as if he knew him. Someone familiar, like Dad perhaps, though he hadn't seen Dad for ages. He had felt breathless, almost disorientated by this strange figment of his imagination and had been relieved when Aunt Dorothy had said, 'That's Tyler, dear. His mother, Leela, teaches him at home, and now he's older, Leela gives him all the freedom he wants. He's just a little strange and never wants to leave this place.'

She had swung the car to the left, through an open gate and into a long drive. They had gone down and down between dark green rhododendron bushes and through wooden gates that Sam opened for his aunt. They had swung round another corner and there it was, an old mansion, standing in a wide valley of grass and sheep.

'Of course it's falling to bits,' Aunt Dorothy had said with a sigh, 'but inheritors can't be choosers.'

'You could say that again,' thought Sam as he inspected his bedroom's brown ceiling and the faded red roses of the old wallpaper. He turned back to the window. In the distance darkness was rubbing out the horizon, merging the edges of the valley with night clouds. Nearby broken down outhouses were full of chickens and dogs and to the left he could just see the muddy enclosure where the wild wounded birds and animals lived. A bit like the mansion, he thought. The words neglected and hopeless came into his head – and noisy. For the night he had arrived, he had heard scuffling noises in the walls, as if the rats had taken over. Or was it someone creeping about?

'Rats? Of course there's rats. They're in the wainscoting,' Chloe had told him the next morning in a matter of fact voice. She had looked at him in a funny way that made him want to slap her face. Why did she think being twelve gave her the right to despise him?

He left the window, sprawled on the bed and opened a book that he had found in his bedroom: **Devon Myths and Mysteries**.

'Kingsholt has its own secret places, its own ghosts, its own under-ground passageways and stone mines, its own stories of the great Christian King, Alfred.'

He read on but it wasn't easy for now the room was full of shadows and the bulb in the table lamp was broken. Typical of this place, he thought and after a while closed the book with a snap. On the cover, Kingsholt library was stamped in gold letters. Sam wondered if Chloe had left it on his bed on purpose, to tell him something about the valley she had moved to, or maybe something about herself. But he wasn't sure, he wasn't sure of anything his cousin did any more.

He went back to the window and stared at the old abandoned barn straight ahead.

At that moment, as he was picturing Chloe as she once was, something went right through him like a force he couldn't resist. It rooted him to the spot, held him down, pulled him, distorted him. It was as if he was being dragged back through time.

He watched helplessly as a round-backed figure in a long robe appeared in front of the barn. It was getting almost dark and the figure was at some distance and yet he could see the man's expression quite clearly. His face was compelling and kind and urgent, as if he wanted to say something but was silenced.

There are centuries between us, thought Sam, the long white curtains of time muffle all sound.

Hey, wait a minute! Where did those words come from?

The monk, for surely that was what he was, smiled gently, lifted his right hand and threw something down. Then he melted into the barn wall, so quick and light he made no noise at all.

Sam didn't know how long he waited for the figure to return. It was only when he saw Aidan striding up towards the barn that he gave up and flung himself on the bed. He had probably imagined the monk in the way he saw other things in his head, his photographic memory firing on all cylinders. Eventually he felt driven to go back to the window. A huge bird was flying in and out of the half-darkness, swinging over the trees and circling down to the barn. This place was too creepy for words. He couldn't stop himself from shouting out and rushing to the door.

'What's the matter then?' called a deep voice from the shadows at the bottom of the stairs. Sam ran down and peered at Aidan. Iron grey hair, tall, with a straight back, he observed, the opposite of the hunched figure he had seen from the window. But he wasn't sure if he should tell Aidan about his over-active imagination, after all, he barely knew him.

'Do you know anything about the trains?' he found himself saying instead, as if he was going to leave any moment.

Aidan laughed. He had a gap between his front teeth that made him look harmless despite his strong appearance. 'Me? Train times? Good Heavens no! Why should I? I never go away. Now tell me, what's the matter? I heard you call out, didn't I?'

They went into the kitchen, a tall room streaked with cobwebs that no one could reach. A silence fell between them and Aidan didn't press Sam to speak. Instead he opened a drawer in the old, green painted dresser and held out a rusty curved object.

'I found this just now, up by the barn. Have a look.'

Sam refused to take it. He didn't want to get caught up! Only yesterday, in an unexpected flash of friendship, Chloe had told him not to get involved with anyone here. No one at all, she had said as she ran out of the room.

Aidan turned the object over and peered at it closely.

'It's for scraping skins – preparing them for writing.'

'I know all about that,' said Sam, surprised that he had something in common with Aidan. 'I've always liked writing.'

'So did King Alfred,' said Aidan. 'Anyway, it's in your family. Uncle George wrote a fine copper plate, and I believe his mother had a good hand.'

'I didn't know writing was genetic.' Sam laughed in relief. He felt himself warming to Aidan. He looked up into the clear grey eyes and spoke casually. 'I don't make a habit of shouting out loud in case you think I do. Quiet and cunning, that's what they say about me. But this was a bit much. I was at the window when I saw this man – don't laugh – looking like a monk in a long robe. Not joking. The thing is,' he spoke hurriedly, 'I don't know if I was daydreaming or not.'

He smiled ruefully. 'I expect you think I'm mad.'

Night clouds were gathering in the sky and Aidan put on the light. His genial face looked suddenly strained. He left the rusty object on the table and put his firm hands on Sam's shoulders. His grey eyes were sharp but kind and Sam felt encouraged. 'I don't know why my aunt and uncle took on this place. It was much better when they spent the summer holidays by the sea. It was cool there.'

Aidan sat down and placed his hands together on the wooden table. He wore a funny expression, as if he wanted to be critical and loyal at the same time. 'When your father walked out, it was the last straw for Uncle George. That's why Kingsholt went to Dorothy and Jack.'

'Just as well my Dad did fall through a black hole,' said Sam emphatically. 'It's a spooky place if you ask me. Why do you stay here?'

Aidan's grey eyes grew intent, as if he was looking at some distant scene.' Maybe it was meant to be. Uncle George and I were both on a retreat at Lindisfarne, for different reasons. As you know, his wife had died many years ago and he had no children. That was something he deeply regretted, so he came up with the idea for a centre for children in trouble. A sort of haven or retreat, where they could find themselves again. He thought he could get funds and professional help. But then,' a sadness came into Aidan's eyes, 'a shadow fell over the valley. It's not called Nimbus for nothing. Half shadow, half halo. That's where Nimbus got his name.' He looked closely at Sam. 'You didn't imagine the monk for nothing.' His hands moved along the edge of the scraper.

'I don't like the sound of that,' said Sam lightly. He paused. 'Chloe's a lost cause, isn't she?' To his surprise the grief was still with him and he looked almost pleadingly at Aidan.

'It's her hair,' he said, mocking his own feelings. 'She used to have good hair, almost down to her knees. Now she looks like something off a scrap heap. Spiky hair and thin as a – I was going to say a ghost!'

Aidan smiled and Sam remembered Chloe's words, 'I cut my hair to look my age, so don't you forget it!' That was yesterday, standing in front of him, her hair jagged, her face pale and sharp and small. Perhaps being twelve did make all the difference after all. Perhaps it was a protest because her mother was always lost somewhere in this huge derelict house and her father was always away. Then there was this weirdo. It was best not to think about it.

Aidan stood up and pushed his chair against the table.

'There's a lot to work out. With God's help.'

'It's nothing to do with me,' said Sam. 'I don't live here, thank goodness.'

At that moment there was a commotion outside the door and Chloe and her mother rushed into the kitchen, shouting at each other. Dorothy looked tired, as if she had had enough. Sam felt sorry for her. He knew how Mum felt after a hard day at work.

Aidan picked up the scraper and gave it to Sam. 'It might come in useful,' he said, 'don't lose it.'

Sam grinned and put it into the back pocket of his jeans. 'If you say so.'

Aidan smiled as he walked past Sam. 'If you're still around tomorrow, you might like to come up to Bones Wood. I've got some clearing to do. Perhaps you could help!'

He went out and closed the door firmly.

Chloe pointed at Sam. 'You don't believe in Aidan, do you? Don't be a dumbo. He's spying up in the woods, that's what he's doing.'

'And you say I have imagination,' said Sam dryly.

Dorothy Penfold frowned and visibly gathered up her strength. 'Enough of that. There's plenty to do without sorting you two out. What about eggs and bacon for supper? All right?'

'I can cook,' said Sam, relieved to talk about something concrete. 'I like cooking. We've got electric at home but I've read all about Aga stoves in Mum's Aga Sagas.'

Dorothy smiled with relief and sprawled in a chair. 'Your mother told me you're a dab hand at all sorts of things – acting, writing calligraphic jam labels, cooking. Well done! It's just as well! Early tomorrow I have to go back to the old house. I'm still sorting it out for the tenants. Jack'll be in London for the week and he wants me up there for a company dinner. Aidan can put his hand to anything, bless him, but it would help if you could cook. I've done a big shop. Leela will sleep in of course, bless her, but she has to go back every evening to cook for Tyler. He's hopeless you know.' She slowly pulled herself up and showed Sam where everything was. 'You two can eat now. I'll get mine later, when I've had a rest.'

'You never used to cook,' said Chloe when her mother had gone. Sam heaved down a large bowl from the shelf. 'By the way, I'm going home tomorrow.'

'You can't!'

'Yes, I can. It's not the same here, not like your old place. As for you, you're a shadow of your old self.'

He hunted round for the eggs and cracked four into the vast bowl that was criss-crossed with little lines.

'Is this all you have?'

Chloe nodded. 'Everything's like that. Big and old. We left all our own things behind for the tenants.'

'And that stuff about Aidan,' said Sam as he beat up the eggs, 'it's sad, see?' He pulled a huge frying pan from a rusty hook on the wall and settled it onto the hot plate. He lined the pan with butter and slipped in bacon and eggs. 'What about fried bread?'

'I suppose so! Do you often cook?'

'Every other day. Anyway, I like it. If I can't be an actor or a scribe, I'm going to run a restaurant.'

'Big ideas!'

Chloe put out some tarnished silver knives and forks and they sat at the long wooden table opposite each other and ate in silence. Chloe picked at her food but Sam ate quickly for despite everything, he was hungry. He was facing the window, wishing he dared to tell Chloe about his out-of-hand imagination. She would laugh at him, he knew she would, even though she'd changed.

Above the trees the grey sky was blotted with red clouds. Now there was no sound outside, except Aidan clanking pails in the yard and the hens clucking round him. Chloe was leaning on her elbows with her knife and fork in the air. The lamplight played on her hair and made it softer. Even her voice was gentler as she spoke, but what she said worried him. 'It's true, everything's changed. In the beginning it seemed wonderful here, out of this world. That was when we first moved.'

She leaned forward. 'I know it sounds crazy, but at night it was so quiet, I thought I could hear singing.'

'What sort of singing?'

'Promise not to laugh. I heard the singing of psalms, chanting, like they did in monasteries. Of course, years ago, there was a monastery built on this land.'

She was looking into her own thoughts now, more like the old Chloe, her eyes dreamy, the colour of those smooth green pebbles they had once found on the beach. Then suddenly she changed again, her eyes sharp, like broken glass. She dug her fork into the fried bread, lifted it in one piece then put it down again.

'If you're not going to stay it doesn't matter,' she said in an offhand way. She scraped the rest of her food into the lined bin and took her plate over to the deep butler sink. She ran a trickle of water over it then propped it up on the big wooden drainer. 'You don't understand. Come to think of it, you don't understand anything.'

'Well tell me then, Miss Know All.'

She sat opposite him and watched him eat another hunk of bread. Her voice was gentle again. 'The first time we came here, I remember the long drive and seeing nothing but trees and rhododendron bushes. I thought we were never going to find the house. Then we turned a corner and there it was, at the bottom of the valley, the loveliest, wildest place I'd ever seen. I didn't think it would ever ever frighten me.'

She hid her face in her hands and when she looked up her pale cheeks were streaked with tears. Sam shoved his hand in his pocket and brought out a tissue. Chloe wiped her eyes, screwed up the tissue and aimed aggressively at the large pedal bin. There was an awkward silence between them and then she said, 'It's not like it was, Sam.'

'Don't be a prat. Got a telly?'

However violent the images, he had always found the world inside that little box was safe. It wasn't like the pictures in your head, you could always switch off what you didn't like. That's what he and Mum did when they'd had a bad day.

'All right,' said Chloe, wiping her cheeks with the back of her hand. She slipped through the door and Sam followed. But first he switched off the light and looked back, just in case.

The high kitchen was full of shadows and the black night clouds almost touched the windows. Everything had become quiet, even the chickens had stopped clucking outside. From here the barn walls looked comfortable and settled where they stood, a little way up the slope. There was nothing now to remind him of the monk. He smiled as he closed the kitchen door behind him. Chloe was calling him into the lounge. Her voice was soft and persistent like it used to be in the old days, a hundred summers ago.

Chapter Six

Chloe shut the front door behind her. The sundial in front of the porch glinted, its shadow-line sharp and thin. Before her, on the grassy slope, sheep were lying, huddled and half asleep under the dark green umbrella of the oak tree, secure in the calm sunshine. As she turned right and walked thoughtfully down to the little river no one else was about. At least Sam hadn't gone yet. As for Nimbus —

For once she felt free of his attractive yet oppressive presence. She leaned over the bridge and watched the green water weed sway with the current. A small dark fish slid above the stony bed, and then another. Fresh water from the hills, Aidan had told her. Millions of years ago the river had gone underground and swirled out caves and caverns that were lost forever. The age-old water and sun relaxed her and she lay back on the grass and was soon asleep.

When she woke, to her astonishment, Nimbus was sitting beside her, staring down at her face.

'It's a beautiful day,' he said, 'and tonight's going to be a good night for stars. Do you know your stars, Chloe Penfold?'

She sat up and looked Nimbus straight in the eye. At first it seemed as if the few days of separation had diminished his power. What harm could there be in him, she thought, he's only hurt and upset and trying to find a way through.

'Why?' she asked.

'We'll star gaze tonight, Chloe. I'll send Tammy down for you, so I don't get tangled up with that cousin of yours, or Aidan. I don't trust either of them one inch, I tell you. The stars will be bright tonight. We'll name them together, you and me and Tammy. No harm in that. We'll see the Plough and Orion and Cassiopeia —'

He looked at her with a soft smile. 'You come out just gone

midnight, when everyone's asleep. Make sure the front door's on the latch and we'll be there waiting for you.'

Chloe nodded. 'All right then.'

It was a clear night and the sky above the valley was steeped in stars. They stood on the highest point of Kingsholt, by the hedge that ringed the valley. To their left was the gate that separated the drive from the road beyond. Nimbus's cottage was in the field below, and to the far side of it was Bones Wood. Below the wood Leela's cottage nestled in black fields. Ahead Kingsholt rose majestically, its dilapidation hidden in the shadows that fell below the starlight. The house was in darkness, Sam and Aidan and Leela were asleep. When Chloe had crept down the main staircase, her parents' bedroom had felt cold and empty, like a tomb, and there had been no noise except the creak of wood. She had opened the great front door as quietly as possible and left it on the latch. They were there, waiting for her and she followed them up into the field.

Nimbus held her hand and aligned her forefinger with the Plough. 'Follow that pointer and you get to the North Star,' he said, 'The North Star never changes. You know all about that, don't you, Tammy.'

Tammy's eyes gleamed in the dark. She was wearing a headband across her forehead and her dress hung loosely down to her feet.

Chloe looked up. The sky was breath-taking above the trees, and the lovely names that Nimbus gave the stars somehow brought them nearer. Something that has a name can't be too far away, thought Chloe. Even Nimbus seemed different under the stars. The lines round his mouth were smoothed out, his forehead was clear as he looked down at her and made sure she under-stood where the stars were and what they were called.

After an hour he said, 'I've taught you a lot and now there's summat you can do for me. I'm looking at Kingsholt, I'm thinking it's a good moment to look round it.'

'Not in the dark,' said Chloe, suddenly shocked.

'Makes no odds in a house.'

'Why don't you come tomorrow?'

'I tried once before,' said Nimbus, 'Aidan Hardy stopped me.' His eyes sharpened. '*He* stops me whenever he can. Now he's asleep, you say?'

She nodded.

'Nimbus has done a lot for you,' said Tammy, tucking her arm into Chloe's, 'and it's not just the stars he wants you to know about.'

They both looked at Chloe and she faltered.

'One or two rooms then, and maybe the others when Aidan's away.'

'He's never away.'

'My mother would show you around.'

Nimbus laughed. 'She's gone away. Come to think of it, she's always going away.'

He flashed his torch as they walked down towards the dark mass of the house. The outline of the roof blocked the sky, but the moon shone on the sundial, the front porch, and on the glass eyes of the stone saluki dog.

'The place is full of secrets,' whispered Nimbus as he urged Chloe towards the front door. She pushed it open and listened to the creak of weathered wood, the groans of old furniture. No one was about.

Nimbus shone his torch on the walls, at the picture of the hunt, muttering under his breath about poor foxes. He flashed his torch at the deerhead and its towering antlers. Then he came to the portrait of Uncle George Penfold and looked at it for a long time, pursing his lips, whispering under his breath, muttering something that sounded like a spell. Uncle George Penfold gazed back, fair and calm in the torchlight, his eyes knowing, as if he was alive.

'You can't stay,' said Chloe peering at him, suddenly feeling she was betraying her uncle. 'There'll be another time.'

Nimbus put his hands on Chloe's shoulders and stared into her eyes. 'We're going upstairs, Chloe,' he said quietly, under his breath. 'We're going to the library.'

Tammy nodded. 'We must all be very quiet,' she whispered.

Chloe climbed the stairs slowly, almost in a trance. Nimbus came behind, always putting his right leg first, but despite his limp, silent, nimble, at any moment ready to break into a run. Tammy followed, her ears sharp for noise. Aidan's bedroom was over the kitchen, in the other part of the house, and Chloe was sure Sam wouldn't be creeping about. He wasn't like that.

'Here we are.'

Nimbus quietly pushed his way into the library and the others followed. 'It's a big room,' he said, carefully closing the door. 'Our cottage would go into this room.'

He turned to Chloe and stared into her eyes. She had no power to resist him when he pushed a white pill into her mouth.

'You'll like that. Better than sweets, aren't they, Tammy? You sit down in front of that mirror while I look around.'

A heaviness came over Chloe and she could scarcely keep her eyes open. She sat on the once plush red seat of the chair, gripping its carved oak arms in an effort to keep awake. Despite all her will power, her eyes closed and she didn't know how much time had passed before Nimbus's deep voice pulled her out of sleep. 'What's this then?'

Chloe yawned and peered at the sheet of paper he was waving in front of her. The handwriting was very small and the drawing neat. 'I don't know. Some sort of map I think. Let me see.' She took the thin, yellowing paper from him and tried to bring her attention to bear on the tiny, faded writing. 'I can't read it. Maybe something about Roman stone mines.' She pushed herself up with difficulty and rubbed her eyes. 'I'm going to bed,' she said. 'And you must go home.'

'Then I'll take this with me and you can tell me all about it another time. Tit for tat, eh, Chloe? I teach you stars and you teach me and Tammy how to read. This might be the map I want.'

Chloe yawned again. 'You must let me have it back.'

Nimbus mumbled as he shoved the piece of paper into his pocket and guided her downstairs.

Chloe opened the front door. How refreshing to see the night sky, she thought. Was it only a few minutes ago I was out there, learning the names that brought the stars closer? But they're not close, she told herself, they're a long way off and between each little light the dark is endless. Her gaze dropped down to the rim of the valley and her mouth went dry. Was that a horseman riding in the shadow? She turned and without saying goodbye shut the heavy door quietly. She climbed the main stairway, ran past the library and up the back stairs to her room on the second floor. The half-moon was at her window. It seemed to watch her undress and slip into bed.

Next morning when Sam and Aidan were out shopping, Chloe followed the path to the wood. She must get that map back at all costs.

Two fields away, Leela was out in her garden, watering her clusters of cottage flowers before going over to Kingsholt. She was wearing a bright orange sari, as if she was trying to outshine the flowers. She looked up and waved. 'You're looking very pale this morning, Chloe. Is there anything I can do to help?' Leela's voice was smooth and calming, with a slight accent that added a lilt to her words.

'I don't know,' said Chloe shortly. She watched Leela deadhead the flowers. 'I can't explain. Everything, I guess.'

Leela stood up and looked at her in astonishment. 'Well! Do you really mean everything?'

'No,' Chloe said shortly. 'It's Nimbus. There's something

going on that's all wrong.'

Leela frowned. 'Kingsholt is a funny place at the moment,' she said. 'It's as if a shadow has fallen on it. There's quite a history you know, or perhaps you don't.'

'I don't want to know,' said Chloe.

Leela picked a marigold and pinned it to her sari. 'You've never settled here because you've come at a bad moment and you're homesick for your old house. But you must be careful, Chloe, you mustn't let anyone or anything take you over. I know what it is. I had a bad experience in London and I might have given up if Uncle George hadn't found me and brought me here. I was the first of his unhappy children! And now, even though he's dead, and there's some sort of shadow over the valley, I believe that shadow can't touch this garden or this cottage. A hermit once lived here and left a legacy of many prayers. You see, I believe in prayers just as I believe in the shadow.' She took Chloe's hand in hers. 'If things go wrong for you, this is where you must come. You won't forget, will you?'

Chloe changed the subject. 'How about Tyler? Doesn't he get lonely?'

'Good heavens, no! He's happy on his own, doing his own thing. The valley's his world, you see, and he seems to be unaffected by any shadow.'

'Is the shadow Nimbus?' asked Chloe directly.

'He's caught up,' said Leela, 'he's part of it. He's dangerous.'

'Everyone's against him,' said Chloe.

'It's a matter of choice,' said Leela, picking another marigold. 'When you stand against something, it's human nature to stand against the people who are part of it.'

'But Nimbus says —'

'He's caught up,' said Leela simply. 'Sorrow, revenge, the darkness they can lead to. He's not alone, Chloe. Kingsholt has a history of sorrow and revenge. But it has a history of light too – monks caring for each other, people offering help during the

Black Death. In the end, it's a matter of choice – though some are under a darker influence than others.'

'I imagine it as Dark Time,' Chloe said suddenly.

Leela smiled. 'You sound like someone from my country. They say we're superstitious but I think we're susceptible to forces beyond ourselves.' She put the marigold in Chloe's hair. 'I hope you don't mind me talking like this. '

'I don't talk to anyone else. Mum's great, but she hasn't a clue.'

'It's often like that,' said Leela gravely. 'You're too close. Your mother and I have a different way of talking. Different words. For instance, I would say you're a passerelle, '

'What's that?'

'It's my own word. A passerelle is someone very sensitive to the past, even though they don't know it. Uncle George Penfold once told me that his mother was like that. Take care, Chloe, the dangers are great.'

'You sound like Aidan,' said Chloe, suddenly sharp, a twinge of fear in her voice. She no longer wanted to listen to Leela. Who knew where such talk would lead? She pulled the flower out of her hair and turned to go.

'Be careful,' said Leela, gentle but firm.

Chloe followed the path through the wood, past the white bony tree where Rosie had been killed, up and up, to the field where Nimbus lived in the pest house. She would get back the map and go straight home. Then she would never see Nimbus again. As she approached his cottage she noticed that a downstairs window was broken and plugged with cardboard. She heard voices shouting and the baby crying. Then Gina came out with the baby in one arm and a duffle bag in the other. Her face wet with tears.

'You keep away,' she said brokenly when she saw Chloe. 'I tell you he's up to no good. His first wife went and I'm going too. Assassino!' She rubbed her head. 'Mi fa male! I'll not go back!'

She opened the back door of the old car that was parked beside the cottage and strapped the baby into a car seat. Then she clambered into the front, drew her long skirt into the tiny space and wound down the window. 'I've had enough. He's changed since his daughter died. He'll go to any lengths...Se ne vada, you go home. I'm clearing out.'

The engine spluttered into life and the car bumped down the track, leaving behind a flag of smoke waving from its broken exhaust pipe.

Nimbus stood in the doorway and watched the car disappear round the corner.

'She'll be back.' He was looking at Chloe so intently she felt powerless. Without a word she followed him through the kitchen to the back room, where a huge television was plugged into the corner. A video game had been inserted and abandoned. A small matchstick figure on the screen was jumping over a wall and back, over a wall and back. Tammy came in from the kitchen.

'She's not my mother,' she said bitterly, 'I never wanted her to live with us. I hope she never comes back.'

'Don't listen to her,' said Nimbus to Chloe. 'Come upstairs.'

He wants me, not his daughter. He wants me.

Chloe followed him up the worn stone steps that spiralled from the back room to a small landing above. Three doors stood almost side by side and Nimbus opened the one on the right. The odd shaped ramshackle room was dominated by a large oak desk that was covered with dust. Its legs were curved and the lid was engraved with Celtic knots.

'An heirloom,' said Nimbus. 'It goes wherever I go.' He opened the lid and took out the map he had found in Kingsholt library.

'I've come to take it back,' said Chloe but Nimbus ignored her. He sat cross-legged on the floor and unfolded the map. Tammy sat opposite, her long black skirt swathed round her. She pointed to the space beside her father, and as Chloe unwillingly knelt down, Nimbus took out a pill and a flask from his hip pocket.

Chloe heard Leela's voice in her head but confronted by Nimbus's intent gaze it had become distant and meaningless. With a sense of daring she put the pill in her mouth and picked up the flask. She expected water and as she took a large swig she watched Nimbus and Tammy exchange glances – one of those conspiratorial looks that turned her into an outsider again and made her wish she was as close to her own father. Then the burning sensation hit her and she felt slightly lightheaded. 'I thought it was water,' she spluttered.

'No one carries water in his hip flask,' said Nimbus. His deep, unfeeling laugh took over the room. 'Come on, sit up! You're going to teach us to read the map, aren't you?'

Chloe swayed and rubbed her eyes. The map seemed at a great distance, a little black and white puzzle on the floor. Nimbus's voice came and went, like a wind that swept over her and brought with it stories of another place and time. He was pointing to locations on the map, telling her what they might be. One description stood out so clearly in Chloe's mind it was as if she was inside the underground domain that Nimbus was describing. All round her were natural passageways hidden deep in the ground, formed by the thrust of an ancient river long since gone. Rocky walls curved overhead, uneven in height, here and there covered with clustered formations and dripping stalactites. The image went and Nimbus's voice grew loud, almost angry, as he shoved the map in front of Chloe. 'Tell us, Chloe, tell us.'

'I don't feel very well.'

'You're meant to be clever, aren't you, reading and writing?'

Nimbus stroked the air with his hands, speaking in a low, even voice until Chloe picked up the map. She talked through her teeth. 'Another time, Nimbus, when I'm well.' She tried to stand up. 'I must go home.'

Nimbus's voice hung over the images that came into her mind, insistent, old as the hills. His right hand cupped Chloe's, his left was clenched over the black pendant. 'It matters Chloe and time is on our side for only a little while. You must help me, as I've helped you.'

Chloe put the map close to her eyes. It grew large and small and there was nothing she could understand.

'The writing's too small.'

Nimbus tightened his grip on her hand.

'You're clever aren't you, you're the clever one.'

Lazy, careless, inattentive were the words she mostly heard in her new school. She smiled as Nimbus looked intently at her. He unclenched his left hand and swayed the black pendant before her, to and fro, to and fro.

Chloe watched the shadow in the corner grow taller than the wall, until it crept over the ceiling above her. She knew that soon the shadow would envelop her unless she spoke, unless she made up an explanation. Her heart beat loudly like some sort of time bomb. Tammy was staring at her with blank eyes and the shadow hung above, ready to drop. She began to talk, hardly aware of what she was saying. It was no longer her own voice that was slipping between her teeth, it was the shadow's that was leaning perilously over her. It sounded sleek and dark in her mouth.

'There's an underground passageway that goes through the Roman mines,' it said in a low dark tone. 'It leads…maybe to death, maybe to treasure. You have to find it for yourself, that's what everybody has to do. A hole, a pit, a place of bones.'

The soft black voice withdrew and Chloe knelt and stared at Nimbus. Passerelle, passerelle. Leela's word echoed in her head.

'What are you doing to me?' she asked.

'Listening, Chloe, that's what I'm doing. No harm in listening.'

With a huge effort Chloe stood up. 'I must take back the map. I'm going home.'

Nimbus towered over her, speaking as if he was doing her an enormous favour, 'No, Chloe, it's my map now, and next time you must tell us more.'

Tammy caught Chloe's arm and pulled her round. 'You haven't heard Nimbus shout, have you, Chloe? He's never shouted at you, has he? Don't be mistaken, Nimbus has power and it doesn't do to abuse it.'

Chloe staggered to the stairs and put her hand out to the wall, holding on to it as she circled down to the television room. The tiny figure was still jumping up and down on the screen. She ran out as fast as she could, terrified Nimbus would come after her. She thought the ruffle in the trees overhead was the shadow, sliding down to envelop her, but it was the buzzard, neck forward, straining, ready to swoop. She froze, as an animal might, until the great bird rose and left behind nothing but a few falling leaves. At that moment, she heard the thud of hooves in her head, the thin neigh of a horse.

Chloe stumbled on, half drugged, half desperate to get out of the wood.

Chapter Seven

'You didn't go then?' shouted Aidan. He was roped to a tall beech and was slowly climbing it by wedging his spiked boots into the bark and leaning back onto a cradle of rope. He edged the rope up the trunk as he moved another step. Peering down he called, 'You climb trees?'

'Not smooth ones,' said Sam. 'I've never seen anyone do this before.'

'There's lots of things here you'll see for the first time,' said Aidan. 'Dangerous things. That's if you're staying.'

Sam kicked the bottom of the tree trunk. 'Always was a slow decision maker! Dorothy gave me the time-table just before she left, in case I want to go.'

A twig crumbled to the ground and Sam watched Aidan concentrate on his climb. An electric saw was attached to his leather belt and when he reached the spreading branches higher up he sat in his cradle and began to saw.

Sam was getting a crick in his neck so he decided to explore. He wouldn't go far, but there were things he would like to find out, despite himself. What danger could there be in such a remote quiet place? It seemed illogical somehow.

He wandered off, making sure to stay within the sound of the saw. The shadows from the trees thickened and the undergrowth broadened out. He felt strangely protected by the thin whine of the blade and might have gone further if he hadn't come across a huge pit surrounded by thorn and holly bushes and tall oak trees.

At that instant, the noise of the saw stopped and for the first time Sam felt insecure. He had thought, unconsciously, of the sound as a string that would lead him out of the wood, but now it had gone, maybe forever! The quiet atmosphere had become threatening, the trees were like creatures who had joined hands and would not let go. They closed in overhead, their matted leaves keeping the earth in shadow. In his momentary panic, Sam stumbled and might have fallen into the pit if the thorn bush that tripped him had not also held him above it. He looked down where the newly dug earth crumbled through flints and tree roots to the bottom. He couldn't make out what was down there but he could smell it, a sludgy, pungent smell, like the dead rat he had once found in the shed at home. The smell engulfed him and he clung to the thorn bush with scratched hands. His heart beat loudly, he felt captured by the smell. He looked up and the trees above the pit shivered. There was the great bird, sitting high and half hidden. For a few moments, although it seemed like hours, Sam's fear was so big he hardly existed, as if he had turned into his fear. Was this what Chloe felt, a terror so strong it made your normal self almost disappear? When once again he heard the high whine of the saw he shouted out with enormous relief, adding, 'I'm not the sort of guy who shouts normally!' He was pleased to know his cry was probably lost among the trees.

He backed out of the thorn bush and began to follow the sound of the saw. For some reason he couldn't make out, he felt as if he had a thousand miles to go. It was as if something weighted down his steps, trying to keep him back – trying to keep him in a time of fear; the same force, perhaps, that had rooted him in the bedroom. He expected to come across something terrible, a battlefield perhaps, or a massacre, and was surprised when he saw Aidan's big haversack and then Aidan himself high up in the tree, striding a branch. Had he gone only a few metres? He sat at a distance on a patch of grass and tried to stop his whole body from shivering.

The sawing noise stopped and at the same time a branch fell, almost in slow motion, through the lower leaves, then crashed quickly to the ground some way off. Sunlight suddenly played at the foot of the tree and Sam found his spirits lifted. He looked up and saw the gap in the trees waving like a bright blue flag. Aidan grinned then slowly descended, spiking his boots into the bark, leaning on his cradle of rope and sliding the noose that held him down and down the smooth tree trunk. When he touched ground he unharnessed himself and came over to Sam.

'Enough for one morning.'

He took out a large handkerchief and wiped the sweat from his face. 'You look as if you need something as well!' He rummaged in his haversack for a bottle of coke and they drank in turn until the bottle was almost empty. Sam wiped his mouth with the back of his hand. Sharing the bottle had somehow turned Aidan into a friend.

'I found this pit, and it smelled awful. I've always had a weak stomach. So has Mum. Once she took me to France for the day and I spent the whole time with my head down the lavatory pan! Don't you notice that smell?'

Aidan nodded gravely. 'It wouldn't be so bad if it was just a smell.'

He packed the bottle away carefully into his haversack. 'You see up there?'

Sam followed the direction of Aidan's pointing finger. The blue gap in the trees cheered him still, even though its light was small and very high.

'I'm bringing in the light. And when I've done that, I'll set about building the chapel, just as Uncle George wanted, on the same site as the old one. I'll make it from the wood and old stones that lie about. Have you noticed them?'

Sam shrugged his shoulders. 'I don't normally go around looking at the ground.'

Aidan laughed. 'Sometimes it's useful. Many of them are from the old chapel. Will you help me?'

At that moment Sam didn't even consider what Aidan meant. The thought of Balham flashed into his head in the shape of the kitchen at home. He could see the table where he ate with Mum and did his homework, and the telly in the corner, perched up on a small table with a pile of videos below. He had a vision of

several of his mates choosing what to play. The sooner he got out
of this one the better.

'I think I'll be going home,' he said quietly.

He helped Aidan push the sawn branches and twigs into a
pile and pack away his tools into the big, hemp haversack that
was already bulging with different objects.

'You never know what you might need,' said Aidan, pulling
out binoculars, string, note books, pencils and a bag of
sandwiches. He re-arranged them round the tools, carefully
secured the haversack and swung it up and over his left
shoulder.

'At least you can stay around for today. I've a little more
work.'

'Okay then.' Sam followed Aidan into the undergrowth.

'I have to notch the next tree.'

They scrambled through shrubs and brambles and, from time
to time, Aidan looked up and back to the patch of light. They
must have moved nearer the pit because Sam caught the stench
of decay and his stomach turned over.

'Too near,' said Aidan, moving back and round. He pushed
through a plantation of new firs and stood staring up at a tall
sycamore. Its leaves patterned the sky so thickly, only small
fingers of blue showed through its layers of green and shadow.
'This one!'

He took out his axe and made a notch in the bark.

Just then there was a loud rush of leaves high above and birds
shot up, invisible save for their cries. Sam thought he saw the
shadow of the great bird behind the leaves but he wasn't sure.

'Do you have eagles round here?' he asked nonchalantly. He
never had been very good at birds.

'Buzzards,' said Aidan flatly. 'That bird up there's a buzzard.
It's a bird of prey, like the eagle.'

'Like Chloe,' Sam joked. 'She's a bird of prey. Yesterday she
went off without telling me, and I never saw her for the rest of

the day. Today she's in hiding again. You know, Aidan, there's no point being here if Chloe's not going to be around. Not that I don't like your company but you have to face it, everything here's a bit strange. At home I've only got car fumes to make me ill! But Chloe – the thing is, I can't come to grips with what's happening here.'

Aidan smiled.

'It isn't funny,' said Sam angrily. 'I mean I come while Mum's away, mainly because she wants me to. My aunt beats a hasty retreat, my uncle's not around as usual and Chloe's turned into a freak. There's a limit to my interest.'

'What's the limit?' asked Aidan evenly.

'How she's carrying on,' he said carelessly, and then to cover his tracks. 'Not that I care.'

He was silent for a while, surprised at the way he was talking to Aidan. But he couldn't seem to stop, as if this tall, grave man would take anything he said, anything at all. So he went on, 'This fear thing, I'd hate to get like Chloe and her weirdo. You must see it's enough to make me want to clear off. I really don't understand what's going on.'

Aidan looked down at him, his expression serious. 'Nimbus may have captured Chloe already,' he said.

He put his axe into his haversack and started to walk away from the tree. 'Come with me and I'll show you.'

Sam followed closely behind. Near the edge of the wood Aidan took out his binoculars and adjusted them. 'Take a look at that field, over there, sloping up behind the trees. Can you see the stone cottage – it looks as if it'll tumble down any minute. The pest house it's called.'

'Aptly named from the sound of it,' said Sam. At first the lens were blurred and he fiddled with the knob. Leaves took on hard, big shapes, a bird looked at him with a sharp eye. He lifted the binoculars until he found the sloping field and the stone cottage. Then he focused on a girl with red hair.

'That's Tammy all right,' whispered Aidan into his ear. 'She's one of the Nimbus tribe. The only one who's left.'

'Nimbus tribe?' Sam put down the binoculars and looked hard at Aidan. 'Sounds like something from the Stone Age!'

Aidan laughed. 'It is a bit like that! When Uncle George came across Nimbus and his family living in a squat, he offered them this cottage. Your uncle was the kindest of men, Sam. He knew Nimbus from years back, when they were both children in the village.'

Aidan looked up at the pest house. 'They live their own kind of life. A law unto themselves you might say. Or unto Nimbus. It's true a lot has happened to make him as he is, but —' Aidan looked sharply at Sam. 'He's dangerous. He's giving Chloe drugs you know.'

'Can't we call the police?'

'First of all, Nimbus will deny it, and then he might precipitate something far worse. We have to be careful.'

Sam shook his head. 'It's like a story.'

'It is a story, a very old story.' Aidan picked up the binoculars and looked through them. After a while he gave them back to Sam. 'What can you see?'

A tall, hefty man in black leather swung into the view finder. That had to be Nimbus himself. Why was he staring like that at Chloe?

'Caught up, that's what they are.' said Aidan.

Sam went on staring at them. 'Caught up in what?'

Aidan sighed and spoke in a voice he seemed to dredge up from another depth. 'You could say it's the darkness of a long ago massacre. You could say it's the darkness that still lingers in the stones round their cottage. It *was* the pest house you see, where they kept people with the plague. Or you could say it's simply human inadequacy. Blame, anger, revenge. A tooth for a tooth, an eye for an eye. And grief of course, at losing Rosie and his wife. The common feelings.'

Sam peered at Aidan over the binoculars. 'What do you mean?'

'They were circus people once but a tragic thing happened.' Aidan stopped abruptly. 'Honestly, Sam, there's no point going on about it if you're leaving. Of course if you stay, it's another matter. You'll learn about it all too soon anyway. You'll have to. *And*, how with God's help, we're going to try to bring it to an end.'

Sam looked through the binoculars again. Nimbus and Tammy had disappeared inside the house. If Chloe went up there again, would she ever come out, he wondered.

'She's in danger,' said Aidan. 'What she needs is a friend, a real friend, to protect her. But if you're going home...'

A real friend! Sam felt in his pocket and brought out the train time-table. If he went this afternoon he'd be home in three and a half hours, door-to-door. He could download his latest game and when Mum came home she would be pleased to see him, safe and sound. Nimbus would be blotted out forever.

And so might Chloe.

Very slowly he folded the timetable into four and gave it to Aidan. 'You keep it for me for the moment. I always lose these things.'

Aidan smiled and put it in his pocket. He squatted down and took out the sandwiches, holding them out to Sam who took one and began to eat. For some reason he couldn't quite make out, he felt relieved.

'There's always hope,' said Aidan, munching vigorously. 'You mustn't forget that, ever. It's one of the great Christian virtues. This valley used to be called the Nimbus Valley and that means light as well as dark. That's how Nimbus got his name. There are ways through, Sam. There are always ways through. We'll go to the library and I'll tell you more.'

Chapter Eight

Sam looked up at the stained glass window above the stairway, the stuffed heads of tiger and deer, the faded oil paintings and the prints of hunting scenes his mother had described. It's another world, he thought, it's as if the whole place is floating into the past.

Aidan was inspecting one of the tigers. 'It was Uncle George's great-grandfather who shot it out in India. He was an officer in the army. You have a long line of soldiers in your family, Sam.'

They went halfway down the hall and stood at the foot of the great stairway in front of the portrait of Uncle George and commented on the sideways tilt of his head, the fair, trimmed moustache, the straight nose, the sharp blue eyes.

'Eyes like yours,' said Aidan.

'And the nose,' said Sam, 'short and straight – like my Dad's.'

'Family likeness!' Aidan laughed. 'And look at this portrait of Uncle George's mother. She was very sensitive to the past. I suppose you could say it runs in the family.'

Her pale face was set on a long neck and slim shoulders, her fair hair drawn back into a bun. The expression in her blue eyes was vulnerable, as if she had experienced something from which she had never quite recovered. Yet it was not an unfocussed expression and Sam felt as if she was directing her gaze on him alone. Like Chloe, he thought, she looks just like Chloe.

Sam wanted to know more about Uncle George. There were plenty of rumours but what had *really* happened to him? How had he died?

They climbed the wide stairway with its carved oak balustrade, past the tall stained glass window that rose above the half landing, and up to the next flight where the stair-carpet became even more threadbare and grey and the walls and ceiling were stained and streaked with dirt and cobwebs. The first landing led to a corridor on the right and they followed it past a couple of doorways to another right bend where there was a heavy oak door. Aidan stopped and took out a bunch of keys from his jeans back pocket. 'If you carry on down this corridor, you get to the back stairs that lead up to your bedroom,' he said, 'but this is where we stop – it's the library.' He selected a big, old key, inserting it into the lock.

Sam was surprised. 'Do you always lock up?'

Aidan shook his head. 'I never used to. A copy of an old map disappeared a few nights ago. It was very valuable to me and it might simply be that I can't see for looking. But I have to be careful, I don't want anything else to go.'

The door creaked open onto a room that was in semi-darkness. Sam stood in the doorway as Aidan drew back the red velvet curtains. Like an explosion, the late afternoon sun shone on rows and rows of books lining the walls. Only the chimney place was free of shelves. Above a white marble surround, a huge, ornate, gilt mirror gleamed with light. Sam saw his own reflection gazing back at him and he turned away to avoid his own squint. 'I feel as if I'm in a public library!'

Aidan laughed. 'It is a bit daunting, isn't it. It was Uncle George's great-grandfather who collected many of the books. Some of them go back a long way.'

Sam scanned the shelves for something interesting but all the books seemed old and untouched. 'How many have *you* read?' he asked.

'Just a few. There's a lot of other things to do here, as you know.'

Aidan went over to the big leather-topped table in front of the chimney place and leafed through a few papers that were neatly stacked beside a pile of hard covered exercise books. He frowned and went through them again, this time more carefully. 'That map must be somewhere. I must have tidied it up. Can you see it anywhere, Sam?'

'What map?'

Aidan didn't give him a direct answer. 'I wish I knew. I no sooner find it than it disappears. It's a copy your grandmother made when she was a young girl.'

'You'd think she would have better things to do.'

'You have to know more of the story,' said Aidan. 'Anyway, it's on an old sheet of paper, and all the places on it are marked with very tiny writing. I'd like to get it back.'

'What are these?' Sam tapped the pile of exercise books.

'Uncle George's diaries. At least *they* haven't gone.' He pulled out a chair and Sam sat on the other side of the table, opposite the ornate mirror. Aidan fumbled in his pocket and brought out his train timetable.

'Do you want it back or shall I keep it?'

'I'll get myself another one,' said Sam, lightly. 'You can give that to Chloe when she needs it.' He paused. 'Is she in real trouble?'

Aidan nodded and Sam walked over to the big window and looked out. The hills behind the house were a clear gold-green but the pest house was out of sight, on the other side of the estate. He walked slowly back to the table. The mirror was gold with the low, straight light of early evening and sunlight skimmed the leather table-top. There was an air of friendliness about the library, as if all the books had good things to say and the possibility of evil seemed a long way off.

'I want to know all about Chloe,' said Sam.

'This story goes back well before her. You have to understand the background or you won't understand what's happening to your cousin.'

'You sound like my history teacher,' said Sam, 'he was always side-tracked. Okay, Aidan, I'm only teasing, I'll be patient.'

Aidan leaned back and put his fingertips together. 'Terrible things and wonderful things have happened here. It all started long ago, in 876 A.D.' He took up a little book. 'This is the first biography of King Alfred. It's by Asser, who dearly loved the great Christian King. Of course, he was one of his bishops, so he might have been biased.'

'What's that to do with it?'

'Patience Sam and forgive the old fashioned English. I'll leave out the irrelevant bits.' Aidan found the right page and began to read slowly.

In the time of the twenty-eighth year of King Alfred's life, the Viking army went to a fortified site called Wareham. King Alfred made a firm treaty with the Vikings and gave them many picked hostages and relics so that they would immediately leave his kingdom. But one night, practising their usual treachery, they broke the treaty, killed all the hostages they had, and turning away, they went unexpectedly to another place called Exeter.'

Aidan looked up. 'It was during that march that I believe they passed the monastery that was once here and sacked it. There's also a legend that Alfred, who was pursuing the Viking army, arrived a few hours too late. The whole place was burning, the treasure had gone and most of the monks were massacred and buried nearby. In some ways that massacre still casts its shadow on our time. How can I explain?'

'I'm a dab hand at monasteries,' interrupted Sam, as if he almost didn't want to hear about any shadow that might be affecting Chloe. 'Let me see.' He began to speak in a sing-song, 'They worked the land, said and sung prayers, studied bibles or copied manuscripts by hand, taught and kept silence.' He stopped and smiled ruefully. 'My mother's keen on all this.'

'King Alfred was keen too,' said Aidan, ' he thought faith and learning walked hand in hand. He kept the belief even when things were really bad for him and he had to live hand to mouth in the Somerset marshes.'

'Are you preaching again?' Sam teased.

Aidan smiled. 'I'm back to our local legends. They say that several monks survived the massacre by hiding in the stone mines. Some of them went off and ended up in the monastery Alfred later built at Athelney. The few who remained erected a wooden home and a chapel up in the field. The legend also tells us that out of gratitude for their survival, they built another chapel in the stone mines. It was to be used as a hiding place for church treasure, if ever the houses of God were destroyed again.'

Sam spoke glibly, 'Henry VIII and the dissolution of the monasteries.'

Aidan was too intent on his thoughts to comment. 'The past hasn't gone,' he said. 'It lives inside us all. It's more powerful than many think, especially for people who have had trauma in their lives.'

'Like the Holocaust?'

'In our century, yes. But even the deeper past can affect us.'

'Are we back to Chloe?'

Aidan looked up. 'Maybe. But we're certainly back to Nimbus. His daughter's death has aroused terrible feelings in him and the past surrounds him with its shadows.'

'Is Chloe going to be all right?' asked Sam quickly. To his shame, he found there were tears in his eyes.

'We're here to help,' said Aidan gently. 'With God's help we won't fail.' He looked hard at Sam. 'Whether you like it or not, you're one of those people who are sensitive to the cusp of time, where past and present meet. Isn't that true?'

Sam pulled a face. He remembered the sightings of his Dad and then there was the monk. Heightened imagination was how he liked to think of it, so reluctantly he said, 'Maybe,' and turned away from the subject. 'It's amazing! I actually don't remember Alfred's dates.'

Aidan laughed. 'So the system does fail from time to time!' He spoke as Sam might. 'Alfred the Great 849-899 A. D. King of Wessex, a Saxon kingdom in southwest England. He became

King of England by defeating the invading Danes and established the over-lordship of the West Saxon royal house. What is more he built the first English fleet, encouraged education, and translated several Latin works into English, becoming the father of English prose history.'

'I won't forget,' said Sam. 'Carry on.'

'There's too much to tell. What matters to us is that when Alfred built first a fort and then a house for monks at Athelney – that's a little to the north of Kingsholt – it's possible he sent monks from there to help rebuild this monastery. Anyway, the second building lasted right up to the time of HenryVIII who, as you know, pillaged and sacked the monasteries all over England, including our one.' Aidan's eyes grew concentrated. 'The legend tells us that one of the books hidden in the underground chapel was a copy of the first fifty psalms, translated by Alfred himself in the last year of his life. He introduced each psalm with a little personal comment.'

'Like what?' asked Sam.

Aidan had a paperback copy of the translation on the desk. 'This is what he wrote about the second psalm.' He looked up. 'Do you really want to know?'

'I wasn't a choir boy for nothing,' said Sam, grinning. 'Anyway I always like to know what people have to say and King Alfred was no mug.'

'There's nothing difficult about this,' said Aidan and began to read.

Psalm 11
The text of the following psalm is called psalmus David, that is 'David's Psalm' in English. It is so called because David in this psalm lamented and complained to the Lord about his enemies, both native and foreign, and about all his troubles. And everyone who sings this psalm does likewise with respect to his own enemies...

'Back to Nimbus,' said Sam.

Aidan nodded. 'I suppose we could take a leaf or two out of Alfred's book. He was a great fighter, as you know. He knew all about enemies and really understood King David's cry for God's help. After all, King David's situation was not unlike his own.'

'The effect of the past again.'

'That's true,' said Aidan, 'but to come back to the present. The only other West Saxon prose version of the first fifty psalms of the Psalter is preserved in a single manuscript, now in Paris, in the Bibliotheque Nationale. It was copied in the mid-eleventh-century. If there *is* a copy here, hidden underground, it makes it very valuable.' He looked up, eyes shining. 'It would help me to build the chapel and repair Kingsholt and maybe fulfil Uncle George's dream, that is, if your parents were in agreement.'

'You sound as if you believe there is a copy,' said Sam, pulling a face.

Aidan looked solemn. 'I really have no idea. What matters now is that Nimbus is sure the book exists and that it's his by rights.'

'There's something about a Roman mine in Devon Myths and Mysteries,' said Sam, thinking he'd better return the book.

Aidan gave him a searching look. 'Now we're on the subject, you might be interested to know that map I've lost is something to do with the stone mines. It may even have had something to do with the so-called treasure.'

'Where did *you* find it?'

'In one of the books but at that moment I didn't have the time to study it.'

'If you're anything like my mother, you might have put it back and forgotten all about it.'

Aidan shook his head. 'I wish I had.' He wandered round the room looking at pictures, staring into the mirror, touching books, as if the room itself held many secrets.

'What's all this got to do with Chloe?' asked Sam.

'Everything,' said Aidan, sitting down again. He leaned over towards Sam, clasping his work-worn hands together. 'I think Nimbus is trying to win over Chloe for his own purposes and if he does, I'm not sure we'll ever get her back.'

'You mean he'll —' The idea was too horrible to voice. 'Honestly, Aidan, it's all rubbish.' Then he remembered Chloe crying and felt confused. 'Anyway, it's her own fault. She's got a mind of her own, hasn't she?'

Listen to this,' said Aidan, purposely opening an old, leather-bound book and leafing through it. 'This is the Chronicle of Kingsholt, an early Victorian translation from Old English. It's a local account of how the Vikings rode into this valley. This is the bit that matters.

The monks who escaped crept back from the woods to bury the dead. They dug a pit and placed the bodies in the mass grave. Some were clothed in their bloodstained, rough woollen garments, others were naked. They said prayers and threw earth over the bodies. It was widespread knowledge that if ever the grave was disturbed a darkness would spread over the valley. A curse.'

'The pit,' said Sam quickly. 'It's open. It stinks.'

Aidan nodded. 'I believe the pit where the monks were buried is the very one Nimbus uses as a refuse dump. It was near the pit that I found Uncle George dead. It's there I want to build a little chapel and bring back the light.'

They sat for a moment in silence. The sun had come out again and was shining through the window on Aidan's head, hallowing his iron grey hair so it looked white, making him insubstantial somehow, and ageless.

'The light against the dark. We must use everything we can.'

'But legends,' said Sam, pulling a face, 'Come off it, Aidan, legends are for fun but they're not true.'

Aidan looked thoughtful. 'Not in our sense of the word. But

they come out of big events and often give some sort of clue to what happened.'

There was a noise outside and Aidan stood up as if someone was watching him over his shoulder. Sam looked round. Was it the sudden dip in sunlight, the cloud that went over the sun? Or the slight wind that started up from nowhere and somehow fluttered in the old velvet curtains. Sam looked away from Aidan and into the mirror. To his surprise he no longer saw a reflection of his own face. The glass was covered in a white mist and he had the strong feeling someone was trying to break through.

'It's this place,' he said, 'it gets you in the end.'

Aidan spoke gently. 'If you're sensitive, as you are, Kingsholt, like many places of trauma, gives you a sort of passport to go into the past.'

'That's news to me,' said Sam, jokingly. 'When my Dad was around, he always kept my passport for me. At least I'm in charge now, or think I am.'

Aidan laughed and took advantage of Sam's apparent good humour. 'Come on, let's go and have some tea.'

But Sam persisted. 'It's this place,' he said again, 'it's creepy. I've never been on two levels at once at home.'

Of course, that wasn't quite true. There was the time he saw Dad standing in his green pyjamas at the bottom of his bed, but that was a different thing altogether. He *needed* Dad.

Aidan interrupted his thoughts. 'Chloe needs you, Sam. And so do I. We must break the darkness and help her.'

'She doesn't have to stay around, she has a mind of her own,' said Sam firmly.

'She's captured,' repeated Aidan.

'She doesn't have to be captured,' said Sam, adding aggressively, 'besides, she looks awful and is awful.' He looked straight at Aidan. 'You *can't* believe those stories,' he said scornfully. 'History's one thing, but they're another.'

Aidan shrugged. 'I believe sometimes, we're given help to

overcome evil through something as small and strange as a legend.'

'But it might not be enough.'

'It might not. But we have to act.'

'How?'

'You must use your good influence on Chloe. And I must build a chapel to God. These two things are intertwined.'

'I don't see how,' said Sam, 'but I'll have a go. Chloe used to be nice and normal, you know. The truth is, her parents don't give her any attention at all and I think that's why she thinks Nimbus is great. He's become her father.'

'I didn't know you went in for analysis, Sam,' said Aidan with lifted eyebrows. 'Anyway, all we can do is to have faith that she'll become her old self again.' He abruptly closed the Book of Kingsholt and put it beside Asser's Life of King Alfred and Uncle George's diaries. He looked tired.

'I think it's time to go.' He strode out of the room.

As Sam stood up a limp darkness drifted over the library, as if a mourning cloth had been spread out and everything had lost its shape and colour. Aidan was already clanking the keys and beckoning him through the door. Sam carefully avoided the mirror as he turned to go. But in his mind he could see the monk with a white, rough woollen cowl drawn over his pale head, and a long, brown quill in his right hand.

Chapter Nine

Chloe stood by the hospital cage, next to Sam. A bird with an injured wing was hopping into a dish of water.

'It'll never survive,' she said.

'Yes it will. Aidan will make sure it does.' Then after a while, 'What's the matter, Chloe? You're so pale you look as if you're going to be sick. I reckon it's all those pills you must be taking. Look, why don't we have some fun?'

She smiled. 'It's not an in word round here.'

'Telling me!'

Chloe turned towards him, the words rushing out as if she was making a confession. 'Leela tells me I'm a passerelle. It's a word she made up. Sounds like a butterfly, doesn't it? But it means sensitive to the past. Like our grandmother.'

Sam studied her silently. Would that account for her pale face, her glazed eyes, her lack of substance, her forgetfulness? Was she in the grip of the black past Aidan had talked about, that hung over the stones and woods, the shrieking massacre that came up from the open pit and infected the bones of the valley? Don't exaggerate, he told himself.

'Should be mentioned on the family tree,' he said lightly. 'Chloe Penfold – passerelle.'

'Shut-up,' she said, pressing her hands against her head.

'Only a joke,' said Sam. 'As a matter of fact, Aidan mentioned it to me. He said it's in the family.'

'You don't understand,' said Chloe petulantly, 'he's not to be trusted. He's the enemy.'

'Well, he's my friend.' Sam looked at Chloe. 'Anyway, whose enemy?'

'It's nothing to do with you.'

Sam waved his hands. 'Okay. All is well, passerelle. Now, like I said, why don't we have some fun for a change.'

'Like we used to,' she said, in a half-mocking voice. 'Exploring the loft. That was your favourite, wasn't it?'

'Why not?' said Sam, 'there's no age barrier, is there?' He put his arm round Chloe. 'Come on, let's go and see what there is to eat.'

Chloe said she couldn't eat lunch and went up to her room. She flung herself on the bed. If only it was like the old times. If only she could forget Nimbus. She wondered why it was so difficult when he was bringing her nothing but misery. Even now she could feel his deep hypnotic gaze, touching her, overwhelming her. The drink and pills made her feel strangely powerful, which was more than she did without them. But she must fight her feelings. *She must get back the map and never see Nimbus again.* Then the other voice started up, the one that felt sorry for an outsider, for she was one herself. *The truth is Mum and Dad simply don't care.*

She forced herself to get up and go to the window. Leela was passing in her yellow sari and at the sight of her, some new innocence stirred in Chloe's heart and mind. It no longer seemed impossible to go up to the attic and play around.

Sam was already up there, looking out of the dusty window. The room was full of junk and boxes and piles done up in string or rope.

He pulled out two puppets from an old box and held them up. Out of the two he chose the red cheeked clown wearing a blue striped trouser suit. He flopped it down on top of the dusty box so that its strings became tangled. Chloe picked up the other puppet and examined its fluffed-out brown hair and spherical grin. She danced it up and down. 'Do you remember how we used to do plays?'

Sam picked up the first clown and undid the knots.

'Hallo,' he said in a squeaky voice, 'I'm a magic clown.'

'And I'm a pear shaped princess,' said Chloe in a light voice. 'I'm lost, I'm lost, I'm lost. Can you tell me the way home?'

'Follow me, Princess.'

Sam danced the puppet all-round the attic, while Chloe followed, skipping her princess over the old luggage and packing cases and back to the window. Sam went down into the dim reaches under the eaves and let his clown slump on the floor. They laughed together at their game. 'Second childhood,' said Sam.

Then something caught Chloe's eye and she opened the window, leaning into its patch of sunlight. When at last she turned round her expression had changed.

'What's the matter?'

'Nothing. I'm going down.'

'What for?'

'There are things you simply don't understand, Sam Penfold. All this prancing about – it's crazy. We're not children anymore.'

'It was just a bit of fun. In short supply these days.'

Chloe made a rush for the door. 'Nimbus is down there waiting for me. I have to get —'

'You're not going!' Sam pulled her back but she struggled free.

'Get out of my way, Sam. You don't understand. You go and play football or something. That's just about your limit.' She ran back to the door and Sam spoke quickly. 'Don't go, Chloe. You can't trust Nimbus. You're a puppet in his hands. Get it? He's caught up!'

'Caught up!' she mocked. 'All right, maybe I'm caught up. Listen, Sam, there's lots of ways of looking at things. There are people in this world who haven't had the privilege of learning to read or write. What's wrong with my helping them?'

'I suppose you're referring to that geriatric hippy who's old enough to be your father. Tell me, Chloe, what's going on between you and him?'

Chloe turned the door handle. 'Okay then, since you ask for it, I'll tell you what's happening. Rosie was my age when she was killed by Uncle George. The truth is Nimbus is in grief. Now

Gina's left with the baby. How do you think he feels about that? He needs help. He needs me. He's about the only person who does.'

'Pull the other one,' said Sam. 'He needs you for what he can get out of you.'

Chloe pointed her finger. 'So you're on Aidan's side.'

'I'm on your side, Chloe, though I can't think why.'

'Nor can I,' she said as she went out.

Sam went over to the window and waited for Chloe to come into sight. Below him, the roof sloped down with tiles missing and ivy poking up and over the edges like green fingers. He could see Bones Wood rising up, the place where Aidan was cutting branches to make his shafts of light, so he could begin to build his chapel. And there was Nimbus's cottage, high on the slope, at the edge of the valley, tiny as a toy house. Soon Chloe would be going inside.

He turned away. This attic is full of secrets, he thought, as he came across a pile of odd things; an old brown silk blouse, a dusty, glass sweet jar, full of silver sand, piles of old books. Then, as he was unknotting the puppets' strings and putting them back into the box, he found a tiny notebook, hidden between the soft sheets of tissue paper. At least this would take his mind off Chloe.

'EMILY PENFOLD 1942' he read with interest. 'RIDDLES FOR REFUGEES.'

Like me, he thought, that's just how I feel; a refugee from London.

The riddles were written carefully, in a fine copperplate.

1) *Where the shadow of the sun*
Falls to East the hunt is on.

2) *Unless beneath the stone*
the clue is found
Dark will rebound.

Mad as Chloe, he thought. He put the puppets and the notebook back in the box and went downstairs. Now he would have to invent something else to stop himself from wanting to strangle Chloe. Leela? But she was busy with the housework, going round the mansion with a feather duster. Tyler might be the answer – Tyler, with his dog Judy and his cow Daisy.

It was better in the open air. The sun splashed across the path and by the time he reached Leela's cottage, he almost felt normal. Judy was peering out of the cowshed, her big pointed ears upright, her tail wagging. Tyler was singing to the cow and Daisy was shuffling in the hay, her bell lightly tinkling.

'Hi!' Tyler nodded to Sam. 'Daisy likes a tune. Can you sing, Sam?'

'I was once in the church choir.'

'She loves a song, does our Daisy. Only I can't sing.'

Sam began to serenade Daisy with Hey Diddle Diddle and when Daisy mooed back they both laughed.

'What about kicking a ball about,' said Sam.

'I'd like that. I'll just finish off here. Where's Chloe?'

'With Nimbus.'

'He's a funny one,' said Tyler as they made their way up to the field, reaching the place where the slope flattened out. 'I see him prowling around.'

'What do you mean?'

'At night. I don't always sleep, so I go out. It's the best way. I've seen him up on the hill there.'

'What does he do?'

Tyler spoke cautiously. 'I'm not sure. I don't go that near. Last night I heard them singing *Ring a ring a roses*.'

'That's a plague rhyme,' said Sam.

'Have the map back? Not yet my dear. We still have things to do.'

Nimbus was sitting cross-legged in front of Chloe, under the black pendant, offering her pills, reaching for his hip flask. She looked away but this time he leaned towards her and as she struggled he roughly poured the liquid down her throat and pressed pills into her mouth. She hated him as he held her tight, staring at her and waiting. There was nothing she could do. Soon the drugs would take effect and it would not be long before she would feel as if she had been with him all her life, as if she was one of his tribe, living in the shelter of a great shadow. She tried to concentrate on a picture of Sam but his laughter and flippancy and freedom seemed a long way away. Tears rolled down her cheeks.

'It seems a pity,' said Nimbus, half to her, half to himself, "you remind me of our Rosie. She was thin and gawky, like a fawn.' He paused then said ominously, 'It has to be done.'

Tammy handed her father the map and he spread it open on the floor. Chloe knelt and waited. She was a passerelle and the shadow would soon come back. Its voice would slip between her tongue and teeth, to tell all the secrets it had picked up through the years.

With the greatest effort she had ever made, as if she knew it was a matter of life and death, she fought the voice of the shadow with all her will power. Her words came out slurred and meaningless, a gibberish she could never have invented in a sane moment. For what seemed a long time, she fought the shadow with a sort of madness, until its ghostly voice was only an echo. But still the voice that came out of her mouth was not her own.

'I am old as the hills and as deep as the night. Hidden in a cavern among caverns, a tunnel among tunnels. I am the secret of the stone-mason monks who made my hiding place and kept it secret. There is only one map to where I am, only a few paths to follow. You may go astray, be strangled by the dry fingers of the underground river that leads beyond the stone mine corridors. Or you may find my treasure house and then be lost.'

Where did the voice come from, or the words? How, despite herself, had she become someone else, floating and obedient, part of the Nimbus tribe that had adopted her? Was she a passerelle to the dark forces? Her eyes were closed and she became aware of a change in Nimbus's tone. He was angry, his distant voice sounding harsh and admonishing. He towered over her and she felt as if she was sinking into the pit, as if the ground was trembling below her and Dark Time was trailing its fingers into the shadows.

'Follow me,' shouted Nimbus, pulling her up. His voice frightened her and she said nothing. She was still drugged and it was a great effort to walk. She had little feeling in her feet and no strength to break away. She knew Nimbus was faster than she was, despite his limp. In her strange state she felt as if she was walking on shadows, with Nimbus in front of her and Tammy behind. Twigs and undergrowth cut past her, soft as birds. The wind sidled up to her and took hold of her arms and when they reached the pit she wondered why Sam had talked about the stench of decay. Tonight there were no smells, only soft shadows, clean shapes, smooth flints. She was numb and blank, as if Nimbus had turned her to stone. It was only when they stopped that she had a vague understanding of where she was.

Nimbus was tying her hands together and pulling her to the edge of the pit.

Chapter Ten

In the kitchen Aidan was stirring soup in a large pot. There was a smell of herbs and potatoes and now Sam felt tired and hungry. He didn't want to think any more about his stupid cousin.

Aidan looked at his watch. 'We'll eat now. If Chloe's not back in an hour, we'll go and find her.'

After the meal Sam washed up, then went over to the window. The light had almost gone, trees and outhouses were black against the grey sky. The trail of stars was still faint and the slowly moving light from an aeroplane crossing the sky looked like a moving planet. There was no sign or sound of Chloe, only the fuss of birds settling down, and the quick stir of a night wind flecking the leaves. Then he heard the sound of running feet.

He opened the side door. 'Tyler! Thank goodness it's you!'

'There's badgers in Bones Wood,' said Tyler, as he stepped over the threshold. 'I thought you might like to see them.'

'Chloe hasn't come back,' he said. 'We have to look for her.'

'I suppose the badgers can wait,' Tyler said slowly.

'Do you mind, Tyler?'

Tyler suddenly smiled widely. 'I'll lead the way. I know this place like the back of my hand.'

Aidan joined in. 'If we can't find her in an hour we'll come back here and call the police. I'll go up to the hill and you two make for the woods.'

For all his weight, Tyler walked silent as a fox. It was Sam who scuffed along behind, tripping up over twigs and stones and leaves. By daylight the path was mud smooth but now it seemed pitted with objects. Tyler waited for Sam to catch up. 'Here's my torch – you'll need it in Bones Wood,' he whispered.

Sounds were sharper in the dark, the owl's hoot hauntingly clear, the rustle of leaves bustling with unseen activity. The light from the torch cast a small golden disk on the way ahead, and soon Sam's eyes grew more accustomed to the dark. The trunks of trees loomed on either side, firm and mysterious, as if they could change into other things. Deep, shadowy patches behind reminded Sam of the caves he had explored at the seaside with Chloe. He put his hand in his pocket and clutched the scraper. Odd how it comforted him, even though it had been buried for more than a thousand years.

A light wind brushed the wood and he pocketed a feather that spiralled down in front of him, brown and delicate in the rough darkness. He felt pleased. It was the flight feather of – he wasn't sure what bird it came from but it would make a quill.

They went deeper into the wood until they reached the Nimbus Tree, stark against the shadows. By the light of his torch Sam caught a glimpse of Rosie's name. He hurried on and then, at the smell of the pit, hung back again.

'It's disgusting!'

Tyler took hold of his arm. 'There's something I want to show you. I think I'm the only person who knows about it.'

'What is it?'

'A door in the pit,' whispered Tyler.

'What door?'

'It leads underground.'

Tyler put his fingers on his lips and Sam lowered his voice.

'We're looking for Chloe, remember. This smell! You don't want me spewing all over you, do you?'

Tyler said solemnly, 'You could put a tissue over your mouth and nose.'

'Point taken, only – I haven't got one. And thanks a million but you can keep yours.' Sam zipped his anorak up to his chin, lifting it over his nose and mouth, but it still didn't hold back the pungent stench of decay, adding to the sense of fear that lurked round the pit.

'Chloe won't be here.'

'She might be,' whispered Tyler, 'it's where Nimbus comes at night.'

As they skirted holly bushes, great oaks, ash and sycamore trees, Sam kept his eyes fixed on Tyler's solid form. A sudden splash of moonlight ghosted the wood, shining through the gap where Aidan had chopped down the highest branches of the sycamore to free the light. Sam thought of the chapel Aidan wanted to build and felt strengthened. He watched Tyler shine his torch over the pit and down to a ledge. 'It's in the chalk face, behind there.'

Sam squinted. 'You could fool me.' He could see the chalky side of the pit and the bushes that grew out at every angle but where was the door? It was probably a figment of Tyler's peculiar imagination. 'We're looking for Chloe,' he said, 'not doing a tour of Kingsholt's state secrets.'

'All right, we'd better get on.'

Tyler led the way to the edge of the wood. Without warning he stopped abruptly and pushed Sam down into the bushes, then crouched down himself. Dark forms were moving towards them in single file: Nimbus, Chloe with her hands tied behind her back and Tammy. Sam tried to get up but Tyler held him down with surprising strength. All Sam could do was to watch Chloe pass. He pushed his thoughts towards her, willing her to turn, but he had to wait for the procession to go round the corner before Tyler let go of him. 'We should've gone for it, you idiot!'

Tyler stuck to his guns. 'If you want to help Chloe it's best Nimbus doesn't know you're here.'

Now Nimbus was moving towards the pit. Behind him, Chloe was dragging her feet and Tammy was pushing her on.

'You got it then?' Nimbus's voice carried across the trees.

Tammy gave her father a piece of paper. Nimbus pushed it at Chloe, forcing her to look at it. 'Is it down there then?'

Chloe was silent.

'She said it was here before,' said Tammy. 'A passageway leading from the pit. That's what she said. Didn't you, Chloe?'

Chloe remained silent.

'That must be Aidan's map,' Sam said, forgetting to whisper.

Nimbus looked up sharply. 'Who's that?' He looked round.

Sam's heart beat fast. *I'm having a nightmare,* he thought. For a moment it seemed as if time had no depth and everything was taking place on the same plane; the day Dad disappeared; the moment Mum stood in the supermarket and cried over a tin of baked beans because Dad used to eat them; the night Dad leaned towards him at the bottom of the bed and the time when he was looking out of the window and the monk waved at him, then disappeared as easily as he had come. He put his hand into his back pocket and touched the scraper. He immediately felt calmer.

Now Nimbus was pushing Chloe forward, through the shadows, and Tammy was following. Very slowly and quietly, Tyler and Sam stalked them, edging their way from one bush to the other until they reached a clump of undergrowth near the edge of the pit. Sam wrenched his anorak over his nose and mouth and peered down. Bottomless shadows lay buried, one on top of the other. Their darkness was filled with scurries of small feet – were they rats and mice who had been feeding on the refuse? His stomach heaved and he clenched his fist round the scraper, willing it to give him all the strength he needed to face this darkness from the past. To his relief he felt a little better. He watched Tammy crawl backwards on all fours and Nimbus move slowly further down into the pit, pulling Chloe behind him, beating the undergrowth with a stick, cursing as he stumbled. He stopped on a ledge of flints and Tyler whispered, 'He's found the iron door!'

There was a faint hollow ring as Nimbus struck the metal with his stick. 'This is it, Chloe, this is what you saw on the map.'

'It's a little bit open,' whispered Tyler. 'I leave it like that so birds won't get trapped inside.'

There was a thud, the sound of breaking twigs, a door

creaking. 'In here,' Nimbus called. 'This is where we'll keep you until you're ready to tell us more about the map. Or until they pay up.'

Sam stood up, enraged. 'You can't,' he shouted angrily.

Nimbus flashed his torch round. 'Who's that?'

Tyler flung Sam to the ground and put his large hand across his mouth.

'We can still stop it,' breathed Sam, through Tyler's thick, hot fingers. 'And you're hurting me. Get off, you dummy!'

But there was nothing he could do against Tyler's solid strength, his big hand clamped over his mouth. When at last Tyler let go Sam clenched his fists and pummelled Tyler's firm body.

'We'll get her back when Nimbus has gone,' said Tyler, pulling away. 'Then he won't know, will he? Then we'll have more time.'

Sam hugged his knees and pressed his face against them in an effort to overcome his feelings. Full of despair and frustration he was unaware of Nimbus climbing up the pit towards them. He only felt a quick surge of pain as Tyler shoved him into a hollow under a bush. He stayed there, immobile and stunned, as Tyler stood up.

'So it was you,' said Nimbus in a sour voice.

'You know me,' said Tyler, ' up half the night. See nothing, say nothing. That's how I am. I've only just got here.'

'What do you mean, see nothing?'

'Mean what I say,' said Tyler fearlessly. 'Only see owls and rabbits and rats and mice and ferrets and badgers That's all I see. Nothing else.'

'Get out,' said Nimbus. 'There's no badger holes round here.'

'There's nothing would live round here,' said Tyler. 'Nothing but rats and mice and ferrets. Is that what you two are looking for?'

'You go on home,' said Nimbus. He turned and put his arm round Tammy. 'This is our refuse pit, so don't you come near it.'

Tyler held his nose between his fingers.

'Get going,' said Nimbus.

Tyler looked up into the dark sky. 'It's the buzzard I'm watching tonight.'

The great bird rose through the dark leaves and for a moment plugged the light shining through the trees. It winged round and curved back into the wood, shivering the leaves, turning them as dark as the shadows in the pit. Tyler slowly followed Nimbus and Tammy, talking loudly of bats and buzzards and the tawny owl he wanted to find. Sam watched them quietly until they disappeared among the trees, then he picked up the torch and crawled out of the hollow.

'I'll stay here,' said Tyler, reappearing, 'keeping a look-out. I'll hoot if there's any sign of Nimbus and hoot twice if he goes away.'

Sam nodded. He was scratched and aching. He pulled his anorak over his nose and mouth and looked into the pit.

Would he dare to go down? Say he slithered to the bottom and could never climb up? Then he thought of Chloe behind the iron door and was sure her horror and fear must be greater than anything he felt.

He tested the slope. It was covered with grasses and small bushes and flints that slipped and took you with them. He crouched down and felt the ground with his hands. Stung by nettles, he pulled the sleeves of his anorak over his fingers. He went slowly, one foot in front of the other, balancing his weight, watching the patch of ground that was always a little way ahead of his feet, so that he wouldn't slip. As he edged toward the bush that hid the iron door, he slid on a strip of loose flints. Shooting out a hand, he caught hold of a branch of the bush, clinging to it with difficulty. Sweat dampened his palms and he was going dizzy. He didn't dare let go, even though his arms were aching and the branch was straining under his weight. It was then, out of nowhere, he saw the monk on the edge of the pit and heard him singing a psalm he remembered from an age ago when he was a choir boy. *Or was it a patch of moonlight and the wind in the trees?* He wasn't sure but he did know that it gave him strength. He forced himself to look up to see what else he could hold. Just above him a small flint ledge, overshadowed by a bush, jutted out and there in the side of the pit, was the iron door. With his free hand he made a grab for the ledge. At first his grip slipped but he tried again and this time held firm. Keeping hold of the branch with one hand, he pulled himself up with the other, surprised at his own strength, he sat on the ledge with his stomach heaving. It was ages before he felt well enough to examine the iron door. When he did, he found it was encrusted in rust and small growths, perhaps the shells of molluscs that had become embedded a million years ago. There was a rusty lock and beside it a strip of deep, black shadow that marked the gap between the door and its jamb. He was able to tuck his fingers into the gap and with his left foot kick at the iron door. At first it would not move and he began to lose heart. Would he ever reach Chloe? He felt in his pockets for the scraper and as he touched it his despondency turned into strength. He wedged it into the gap and with renewed energy levered the door until it creaked and swung inwards. He'd done it! A surge of triumph washed over him as he switched on the torch and went inside.

He had expected to find a small, overgrown place, a hole full of vegetation and water. Instead he was facing a man-made tunnel that curved over his head, and sloped up into the hillside. It was carved out of the natural stone. Sam shone his torch onto a clump of bats that were clinging to the hacked-out ceiling. He must be in the Roman stone mines, he thought, with a sudden sense of adventure.

Chloe was lying on her side, a little beyond the first corner. She was gagged. Her hands were loosely tied and her feet were roped together. As Sam undid the gag Chloe groaned.

'Don't you worry,' said Sam, 'I'll get you out whatever happens.' He shone the torch onto her feet and with difficulty prised open the knots, then he struggled to untie her hands. Once again he had the strange feeling he was in a time warp, as if he and Chloe were wedged into some sort of no-man's land, where nothing and infinity were intertwined. Was it the darkness that gave him this strange sense of floating down through history?

After what seemed an age, yet no time at all, Chloe slowly sat up. She shook as she rubbed her arms and feet. 'Oh Sam!'

He put his arms round her. 'It must've been awful.'

She clung to him. 'I had this dreadful nightmare,' she said in a hoarse voice. 'Dark Time came down from there.' She pointed to the slope. 'His horse neighed as he bent over me and tried to make me ride with him into the darkness.'

Sam shuddered, holding her close. 'It's all right, it's all right. I'll soon get you out.'

He half held, half dragged her to the end of the tunnel. He heaved against the door and when it opened Chloe collapsed on the flint ledge. Sam realised there was little chance of climbing out of the pit on their own.

He didn't know how long they stayed there under the bush. The full moon climbed from one branch of a tree to the next, turning Chloe's skin paler than ever. There was no wind and the ghostly light made the chalky flints look insubstantial, like feathers. The high leaves were whitish in the moon but below there were hollows of darkness and Sam wondered if Nimbus had crept back and was spying on them, unseen, ready to ambush them. When he heard the creak of branches he stiffened, trying to see through the black leaves.

A figure appeared at the top of the pit and another behind. Sam cowered down next to Chloe, hoping the bush was thick enough to cover them both.

'There, behind the brambles.'

His heart turned over, but with relief, not fear. Surely that was Tyler's voice and the tall straight figure beside him was Aidan, not Nimbus?

He stood up, almost dislodging Chloe as he did so. 'We're stuck,' he whispered between cupped hands.

Aidan came down sideways, clinging with his fingers where the slope was too slippery. He stopped just above them and untied a rope from round his waist, throwing one end silently down to Sam, who looped it round Chloe. Then Aidan pulled her up the slope, little by little, while Sam wedged his feet into the loose flints and pushed her from behind.

Out of the darkness, Tyler hooted, once, like an owl, and Aidan signalled to Sam and Chloe to lie flat on their faces against the pit. The undergrowth rustled, the wind swept up through the trees like a great invisible bird. Then, in a renewed moment of silence, Tyler hooted the all clear and they resumed their climb, edging their way slowly towards the rim of holly bushes.

'Nimbus is on the prowl,' whispered Aidan. 'We must be careful. He's obsessed! He's mad! I don't know what he'd do if he found us.'

Chapter Eleven

Sam and Aidan supported Chloe as Tyler led them silently down a hidden track that ran through the undergrowth and out to the field below. Moonlight flooded the long grass.

'She's back,' said Aidan, pointing to a light from Leela's cottage. 'I told her to go home and wait for us there.'

'Mum knows *I'm* all right,' said Tyler placidly,' she knows no one harms *me*.'

As he was speaking Chloe slumped and collapsed into the grass. Aidan picked her up and carried her in his arms.

'She's light, too light.'

A shaft of yellow dropped from the front door and Leela stood there, her hands shielding her eyes, looking out into the dark.

'Is that you, Tyler?'

Tyler strode ahead. 'Me, and the others,' he called.

'You all look exhausted,' said Leela as they crowded on the doorstep. 'Come in quickly, before you're seen.'

There was a noise from the wood, shouts, and a cry that rose and fell. Out of the dark line of trees the buzzard flew, circled round and swept back into darkness. Leela hurried everyone inside and closed the door.

Sam looked round. It seemed a long time since he had been in such a warm and cheerful room. The carpet was a soft moss green, threadbare in parts, the curtains and rickety couch were in a bright cherry blossom pattern. The low ceiling was crossed with two old timbers and from a beam above the wide fireplace a bunch of dried flowers dangled beside a silver pendant and a copper kettle. A sense of relief relaxed him, he had the feeling no-one, not even Nimbus, could harm him here. Aidan settled Chloe on the couch where she lay limp and fragile.

'You've had enough, poor thing,' said Leela. 'I'll have to help you change your clothes. They're damp and they smell of mildew.'

Aidan and Sam moved away as Leela helped to undress Chloe.

'I have the very thing,' she said, presenting Chloe with one of her own night gowns.

'It's too beautiful,' said Chloe softly. 'I usually wear a tee-shirt.'

Leela smiled. 'Just you rest and get warm now,' she said, covering her with a deep blue duvet.

'I'm all right,' said Chloe, 'really I am.'

'She's not,' said Sam, 'she needs a doctor,'

Chloe sat up slowly, hugging the duvet close to her.

'I fought him. I tried hard. I know that, though I can't remember everything.'

'What happened?' Leela asked gently.

'I don't know.' Chloe slumped back onto the couch. Tears trickled down her cheeks. 'I'll be all right. I just need sleep.'

'If you're not all right in the morning, I *will* call the doctor,' said Leela. 'What about a hot cocoa and oatmeal biscuits? Then you can all settle down on sleeping bags. You'll all be safe here.'

'It's good of you,' said Aidan. 'Everyone needs a rest, though I'll stay on guard. You never know.'

That night Sam shared Tyler's room.

'You have the bed,' said Tyler, turfing off Judy and wriggling down into the sleeping bag he had placed on the floor underneath the window. He leaned up on his elbow to talk.

'I didn't want to leave you up in Bones Wood but I knew it would be best if I went straight back for Aidan and told him everything. He was so worried he tried to phone Chloe's parents to tell them to come back.'

'Did he get them?'

'There was an answer phone saying they were so tired they had gone off for a little break together and would be back next week.'

'That figures,' said Sam angrily. 'Of course, Aunt Dorothy finds it hard to cope at the best of times.'

Tyler nodded. 'Aidan thought of phoning the police but he was afraid they'd question Chloe and that was the last thing she needs at the moment. So he grabbed his haversack and we came as quickly as we could.'

Sam grinned. 'Just as well he takes all that stuff with him. Without the rope we'd never have got Chloe out of the pit.'

'He's on guard tonight,' said Tyler, 'but there's no need. No one comes here. Nimbus has never been here. Never.'

He yawned and pushed down into his sleeping bag.

'There's always a first time!' said Sam but the sense of relief stayed with him. Chloe was safe below and Aidan was in the kitchen, keeping watch.

Moonlight smudged the windowpane and the thin flowery curtains shielded them from the night. Yet in his mind he was still out there, scrambling down the pit, opening the iron door, finding Chloe in the tall man-made tunnel. Now he was going down the tunnel, down and down and down into the dark world of the Roman mines.

Before he knew where he was, he was fast asleep.

In the morning a grey bristle covered Aidan's jaw line and shadows lined his eyes. Sam looked at him with admiration. 'Were you up all night?' he asked over breakfast.

Aidan shoved a forkful of bacon into his mouth.

'More or less,' he said. 'Nimbus was prowling about like a wild cat. He knows Chloe's gone.'

'I think it best if she stays here with me,' said Leela, putting three sizzling pieces of bacon on Sam's plate. 'She's still fast asleep, bless her.' She turned back to the stove. 'If only we could get in touch with her parents. They could take her away. Didn't they leave an address?' She sounded puzzled.

'No!' said Aidan. 'They obviously trusted us completely.'

Leela poured the tea from a big blue tea-pot that had seen better days. 'Well, there you are. I'll stay here with Chloe and see how she is when she wakes up.'

'If you like, I'll sleep over at Kingsholt,' said Tyler slowly, 'then Chloe can have my bed.'

Leela, looked at Tyler, her eyes dark and bright. 'Would that be all right, Aidan?''

'I'll take the football with me,' said Tyler, now that he had decided what to do. 'Judy'll come as well.'

'You're more than welcome,' said Aidan. 'We're going to need you in every way.' He looked round at the small group. 'I don't think we have enough evidence to call in the police yet. I can hear Nimbus denying everything and making more terrible accusations. I also think Chloe, despite everything, would say there was nothing wrong.'

'How *could* she?' said Sam.

'It's possible Nimbus drugged her,' said Aidan briefly. 'It's true she's begun the good fight back but it might not be enough. It's a difficult situation but for the moment I think it's best if we manage on our own.' He turned to Leela. 'You stay here with Chloe but it would be useful if you could come over to Kingsholt – say tomorrow morning – to keep in touch and make sure everything's in order and tell us about Chloe.' He turned to Sam and Tyler. 'I want you two to keep an eye open. It might be an idea if you kick a ball about and have a look round. If you see or hear anything of Nimbus or Tammy you must let me know. I'll be up in the woods sawing branches. I'll have a good view from there.' He looked grave. 'Nimbus'll stop at nothing now he's lost Chloe. He kidnapped her to bargain with us and now he hasn't got her, he'll either try to find her or go after the 'treasure' on his own.'

'How can he?' said Sam.

'I believe he's got the right map,' said Aidan quietly. 'Whether he can read it or not is another matter. So please pray. We need help to sort it all out, and that's the moment we'll call the police if we have to.'

Sam buttered a large chunk of bread and ate it slowly. This morning he was less afraid than he had been last night and yet he was haunted by what he might have to do. He had no means of defending himself. Unlike Aidan, he carried nothing in his pockets, or nearly nothing. He emptied them out. In the face of danger, what good was a scraper and a brown feather? Yet for some reason he felt unwilling to part with them. Words from nowhere came into his head. *They keep me in touch with that past world, when the valley was filled with the singing of psalms.*

Leela gave him a shrewd look. She went out of the room and came back with a small brown bottle in a plastic bag. 'Now this should take your mind off things,' she said. 'It's a small present. Can you guess what it is?'

Sam unscrewed the lid and smelt the brown liquid. 'Nice smell. Oak gall ink?'

Leela smiled. 'You're right. And there's quite a story to it.

A long time ago, when I was decorating the cottage, I was scraping the wallpaper in the hall and I found a door and some stone steps leading to a cellar. Behind the door there was an old shopping bag with this ink inside it, and —' she nodded at the fireplace, 'I also found the silver pendant and one or two other things, maybe put there for safekeeping by one of the family. Perhaps your grandmother, Emily Penfold...'

'Did you ever explore the cellar? asked Sam.

Leela shook her head. 'I kept the door locked and threw away the key. After all, I didn't want little Tyler wandering down there, did I?' She looked thoughtful. 'The story might be of use. Uncle George told me that a hermit once lived here and used a passage from the cellar to the stone mines. But I don't know.' She poured out some more tea for Aidan.

'Anyway,' she said, 'don't dwell on these things, Sam. My point is that if you do your calligraphy, it'll take your mind off what happened last night. You could make a quill out of that feather in your pocket. There's nothing like a craft to keep the mind calm. I do rugs myself.'

'Thanks, Leela. 'Sam smelled the concoction again. 'Yes, it is made of oak galls. That's what the scribes used.' He screwed the lid back on and carefully put the bottle into the plastic bag, shoving it into his pocket along with his other useless things. He smiled at Leela. He was already feeling more normal and looking forward to kicking a ball around. At least it would remind him of the lads back home.

That afternoon, when Sam and Tyler were playing 'Look out' football, as they called it, Tyler kicked the ball up so high it landed in the wood. He ran to get it then came back to Sam. 'It's Tammy. She's watching us.'

'Spying on us,' said Sam loudly, as he walked slowly towards the wood. Tammy came out of hiding and leaned against a tree as if she had been there all the time.

She defiantly opened a string bag that hung round her neck, took out a packet of rolled cigarettes and offered one slyly to Tyler.

'Don't you take that,' said Sam, as Tyler leaned forward, ready to take whatever was offered to him.

Tammy lit up and blew a ring of smoke into the air.

'Findings keepings, that's what we say.'

'What are you talking about?'

'You'll find out soon enough, Sam Penfold.'

She puffed another circle of smoke up into the trees.

'Nimbus can make people disappear.'

'But he can't bring them back,' said Sam.

Tammy's eyes went blank. She spoke in a softer voice, half to herself. 'It's true. For all his powers, he'll never bring Rosie back.'

Then she smirked. 'There's no stopping him now.'

'Stopping him from what?'

Tammy threw the cigarette down and scrunched it with her heel. 'You don't know anything do you, Sam Penfold? Well, let me tell you this: Nimbus has the map and he'll have his revenge very soon. You'll see.'

'Sam's hand went up but Tyler caught it and held on.

'Come on, let's get back to football.'

'That's all you two are fit for,' said Tammy. 'You wait. Nimbus says before tomorrow's out, he'll have everything he wants.'

Sam made another lunge for Tammy but Tyler took hold of his shoulders and forced him down the slope.

'Let go!'

'If you touch her you'll be in trouble,' said Tyler urgently.

At that moment they were distracted by a noise that was coming from the wood, a high clear whine.

'That's Aidan,' said Sam.' We should report back.'

They went through the trees, with Judy straying and returning, following old tracks and scents. A slight wind rose and carried the smell of the pit through the air. It seemed worse somehow, now sunlight packed the wood and there wasn't a cloud in the sky.

They found Aidan high up in an oak tree, secure in his spiked boots and his cradle of rope. He was sawing at a branch with such speed and concentration he didn't see they were there.

Sam looked round. The afternoon sunlight already pierced the pit, turning the vegetation gold and the flints silver.

Then Aidan caught sight of them and shouted, 'Keep back!"

Another branch crashed into the undergrowth and from the gap in the fork of the trees the sun blazed in a circle of gold. Without forewarning, one of those timeless moments suddenly overtook them. 'I feel breathless,' said Sam as he became aware of something greater than himself.

'That's where we'll build the chapel,' shouted Aidan, his whole face lighting up, 'and that's where we'll sing again.'

At that moment a shaft of light pierced the pit like a sword.

Chapter Twelve

Tyler and Sam sat down and watched Aidan saw off more branches. Now the late afternoon sunlight swayed with the grass and bushes, rippling over the stones, gathering itself up into low shafts of light, until a cloud cut into the sun and everything gold slipped into shadow.

'That's no cloud,' Tyler told Sam, 'that's the old buzzard. He'll swoop soon if Nimbus has left meat in the pit.'

As he spoke the buzzard flew down, picked something up in its hooked beak and swung up again into the trees.

Tyler squinted. 'Dead rat – that's what it looks like.'

There was a rustle in the leaves as the bird flew off to a quieter place.

Then the low sun re-appeared, casting a halo round the valley.

As they all made their way home, Sam told Aidan what Tammy had talked about.

'I thought it must've been Nimbus who took the map from the library!' said Aidan. 'I don't suppose Chloe could do much about it.'

When they reached home, they sat round the kitchen table eating cheese sandwiches. 'Nothing like food to get the brain cells going,' said Sam. 'The next puzzle is: Does Nimbus know what the map means? Chloe told me he can't read.'

Aidan handed out diet cokes. 'It depends how much Chloe was forced to cooperate,' he said thoughtfully.

Sam took a gulp and looked up sharply. 'Tammy said Chloe told him what the map meant.'

Aidan took a long drink from his coke can. 'It depends what you mean by that. It's more likely that Nimbus put her in a trance – after all he was a hypnotist by trade. In that sort of state you sometimes know what you don't know.'

'That would come in useful before exams.' Sam laughed and

reluctantly chucked the last bite of his sandwich to Judy, who was looking up at him hopefully. 'Chloe's safe with Leela, isn't she?'

Aidan smiled. 'As safe as she could be with anyone. But we can't afford to wait. We've got to do something soon. Otherwise Nimbus may find whatever there is and then who knows what he would do?' He looked hard at Sam. 'But there again, I don't know how we'll get anywhere without a map.'

'Why don't we ask Chloe?' said Sam. 'She'll remember.'

Aidan shook his head. 'Not now, I doubt if she'll remember anything now.'

'Why not?'

'Nimbus will have made sure she won't.'

'And I can't help,' said Tyler dolefully, 'I don't know anything about that sort of thing.'

Aidan smiled. 'You're a walking map, Tyler. You know more about the valley than anyone else. Come on, we'll go up to the library. We'll turn ourselves into a think-tank. One of us is sure to come up with something.'

The library was flooded with low sunlight and the mirror caught the late sun, turning it into a burning jewel. Now he had eaten something, Sam felt renewed. Aidan pointed to the highest shelf opposite the mirror. 'I found the map at the back of those books – inside an old ledger.'

'How did you know it might be there?' asked Sam.

'I didn't,' said Aidan. 'I was going through Uncle George's diaries and I came across a reference to his mother, Emily. Apparently she used to copy her father's accounts into a ledger in her beautiful, small handwriting. Then I came across the ledger just before you arrived, Sam. It was hidden behind some of the books, up there, on the highest shelf. Emily's notes were at the back of the accounts with the map that Nimbus took. I think she must have copied it from a much older map.'

Aidan flicked over the pages of one of the diaries. 'Here we are. A page of Emily's writing, stuck in by Uncle George in memory of her.'

Sam looked at it closely. 'What were her notes about?'

'About the Viking raids and about King Alfred. Like me, Emily had a great interest in him, especially because of the local legends. She was sure the name Kingsholt referred to King Alfred.'

Sam jumped up. 'I've just had a thought.' He saluted Aidan as he reached the door. 'Sherlock Holmes at the ready!'

He rushed up to the attic and opened the puppet box. He took out the little notebook and ran back to the library. 'Here we are. Another Emily Penfold thing.'

Aidan examined it carefully. 'It's the same writing,' he said, 'small and beautiful.' He looked up. 'Rather like yours, Sam. Well done! I must say, I didn't think about looking in the attic.'

Sam leaned over Aidan's shoulder and spoke in a deep Sherlock Holmes voice.

> *'Where the shadow of the sun*
> *Falls to East the Hunt is on.*
> Then
> *Unless the book is found*
> *Underneath the stone*
> *Darkness will rebound*
> *From the pitted ground.*

'Sounds like a couple of childish riddles,' said Aidan.

'It won't be a game, Aidan.' Tyler spoke urgently. 'If Emily Penfold knew the valley like I do, she wouldn't play games with its legends. There's something she knows.'

Aidan looked up at Sam. 'Did you find anything else?'

He shook his head.

'This may be enough,' said Aidan. 'I'll try and work it out. You two take a break. There's nothing more we can do today.'

Sam and Tyler went back to the attic and poked around but there were no more clues. Tyler decided to take Judy for a walk but Sam stayed in the attic to make sure he had not missed anything that would help. He found nothing so he took the jar of silver sand downstairs and emptied it into one of the big iron pans. He put it into the top oven of the Aga. By now Tyler had come back and he watched Sam in astonishment.

'I haven't gone mad,' said Sam, 'I'm going to make a quill. First I have to soak the feather. Then I'll strip it and cover it with the hot sand to harden it. Then I'll cut the nib.'

Leela was right. There was nothing like doing something practical to sort yourself out. He was definitely feeling better.

That night Tyler and Judy slept in Sam's bed and Sam settled down in an old sleeping bag that had once belonged to Uncle George. He woke about four o'clock, haunted by a nightmare; Nimbus was tying Chloe to the Nimbus Tree and Uncle George was bound to another tree. Uncle George was in green pyjamas and was shaking his head like some old puppet! Sam felt the walls close in on him so he slithered out of the bag, crept out of the room, along the corridor and past the library where a light was still on. He ran down the main stairway, opened the front door and stepped into the garden. That was better! He breathed in the cool night air.

Moonlight flecked the sheep and – Sam tried to find the right word – *tampered* with the sundial. Without warning, it swam out of focus and took on the shape of the ghostly monk who was pointing above the porch to the saluki dog. Sam looked away and then back, and to his relief the monk had disappeared and the sundial was standing firm again, silvery in the moonlight. Was this some sort of a message? Of course! The sundial was where the sun's shadow fell! This must be the place!

The moon slid behind a little cloud as he ran back into the house and up to his bedroom.

'Tyler, wake up, it's important.'

Tyler groaned and yawned.

'Come on, there's no time to waste.'

Tyler clambered out of bed and pulled on his trousers and old jumper. He and Judy followed Sam downstairs and out into the drive.

'Where's east from here?' asked Sam, standing by the sundial.

Tyler pointed to the stars. 'Let me see. There's the plough and there's the North Star. East is in front of us.'

Sam peered over the flagstones. Little flowers and moss were pushing up in the cracks.

'Somewhere here,' he said, 'that's where we have to dig for the map.'

Tyler looked at him with an open mouth. 'What *now*?'

'If we wait until morning it might be too late. There's spades and garden forks in the lobby. I'll get Aidan.'

Tyler yawned again. 'It doesn't seem right to wake him up,' he said.

'He's already awake,' said Sam.

It took the three of them an hour to lift the paving stones and dig down and another hour to find out there was nothing there. Aidan sat back and wiped his forehead. 'It was a game after all. Emily Penfold was having everyone on. I've already spent too much time on those riddles and I still can't make head or tail of them. Let's face it, she was only a little girl having fun.'

Sam looked at the oak front door and the pediment and the dog who appeared whitish against the dark sky. It was standing like any hunting dog, nose in the air, long legs stretched, barrel chest ready to bear the breath of its speed. Sam knew it was mad, but he had a strong feeling the dog was also part of it. Emily Penfold's riddle beat in his head.

> *Where the shadow of the sun*
> *Falls to East the Hunt is on.'*

'Of course, *that's* where we should be digging,' he said urgently, 'under the dog. The sun's shadow falls there when the sun goes over the roof. I wasn't thinking hard enough.' Or taking notice of the monk, he thought. 'Don't you see, the dog is a hunting dog and the words *'the hunt is on'* is a reminder, isn't it? The dog's a hunter and so are we. We were wide of the mark, that was all.'

Aidan looked tired. 'Sam, you had a nightmare. You have an over-active imagination. You need a proper rest.'

'Please, Aidan. *Please.'*

'I've been trying to remember the map,' said Aidan. ''I've put bits together. It'll probably be enough.'

'Please, Aidan.' Sam looked into his friend's tired, grey eyes. 'It's worth a try.'

Dawn was breaking behind the house. They stood in silence and at last Aidan said, 'All right.' He turned to Tyler. 'You keep a lookout for Nimbus. It's nearly morning and God knows what he's up to. We've been too long as it is.'

Tyler went off and Sam and Aidan dug in front of the flagstones of the porch. Here the ground was lightly sprinkled with gravel and was easily dug. They worked quietly, piling up the black earth into a tumbling mound.

By now the sun was climbing the sky and they were about to abandon the project when Sam's spade struck something hard.

'A flint,' he said, but he wasn't sure. It didn't sound like a flint. Aidan loosened the soil and a black metal edge upended onto his spade. He prised the edge and lifted out a small metal box. 'Fill in the earth,' he said, 'as quickly as possible.'

They were just finishing when Tyler hooted like an owl and then again, urgently.

'Come on,' said Aidan softly.

They went inside and clambered upstairs to the library.

'What about Tyler?' said Sam.

'He'll be all right. 'He'll act as a decoy, leading Nimbus away. That's what he did last time.'

In the library, Aidan spread out some newspaper on the oak table and rubbed the earth off the box. It was an old sweet tin marked with the legend: *Suppliers to King George VI*. Inside was a leather package, protecting a piece of off-cut vellum. It was a map decorated with anchor crosses and old words in an ancient script.

'We've done it,' said Sam jubilantly. 'Nimbus'll never win.'

'Never is a big word,' said Aidan but Sam hardly heard him. The word 'never' kept going through his mind. Never. Never. It was a powerful word, a barrier against Nimbus, against his spells, his murderous intentions. It was a barrier he could put round Chloe to keep her safe, to stop her from ever returning to the pest house on the hill.

'Back to bed,' said Aidan. 'We must have some sleep.'

In the morning Aidan took out a pencil and began to copy the old map, putting all the information into straightforward English. Sam watched him closely, especially when Aidan pointed at two marks. 'You know, Sam, I don't remember any anchor crosses on the other copy. But here's a cross near Leela's cottage and here's one by Blackburr Fort. They might indicate ways into the underground mines.'

Sam yawned. 'I think I need breakfast.'

Aidan ignored him. 'One thing is certain. This *is* a ninth century map of the stone mines showing the position of an underground chapel. I can date it from the script. So at least there's something in the legend.'

'Mum's got an anchor cross,' said a sleepy voice. Tyler was standing by the door with tousled hair and clothes crumpled. Judy was beside him sniffing the air.

Aidan smiled. 'Did you get *any* sleep?'

'Four hours,' said Tyler.

Aidan locked the precious piece of vellum in a drawer of the desk, then gave his copy to Sam.

'Study this. The thing is, we have to act fairly quickly if we're going to find the chapel and bring back anything that might be there. I've marked the route in red but we may have to use our initiative.'

'I'm not going underground without Judy,' said Tyler.

Aidan nodded and opened his haversack. 'Keep my copy of the map in here, Sam, and take the haversack with you. I've put in a pencil and a piece of chalk. You never know, they might come in useful.' He looked up. 'Okay boys, breakfast time.'

They sat round the table while Aidan cooked eggs and bacon and made coffee. They ate in silence.

'I feel better now,' said Sam, wiping his mouth with a piece of kitchen towel. He pushed back his chair and got to his feet. 'Right,' he said, shouldering the haversack. 'Let's get sorted.'

Chapter Thirteen

Chloe leaned on the windowsill, looking out at the field. It was past noon and the air was heavy with sunshine. She opened the small top window and breathed in the garden scents, watching the brown, meadow butterflies dart past as if they, like her, had nowhere particular to go. 'How long was I asleep?'

Leela put her hands on Chloe's shoulders. 'It wasn't all sleep my dear. The first night and the first day you were in some sort of trance. I don't suppose you remember much about it. But last night you slept well and now you look so much better, especially since you had breakfast.'

'What's the time, Leela?'

'About ten o'clock. I promised Aidan to look in at Kingsholt, to make sure that all is well. But I won't be long, Chloe and there's no need for you to get dressed.' Leela smiled. 'You may even want to go to sleep again.'

'I like sitting here, looking out.' Chloe patted the lacy gown that Leela had given her to wear. It was very old, Leela said, there was no counting the years. She had found it when she was decorating. It was in a bag, hanging on a door concealed behind wallpaper, that lead down to the cellar.

'You're the first one to wear the dress,' she said. 'And it's not the only thing I found. Look at this.'

Leela hung a silver pendant round Chloe's neck.

'It's very old, based on a Roman sign. The anchor cross is what they call it. You keep it with you now.'

When Leela had gone, Chloe looked at herself in the long mirror that hung on the wall beside the window. The touch of lace on the voluminous, white linen gown made her look like someone from another age. She took it off, washed and dressed in her clean jeans and tee-shirt, then lay back on the bed with her arms behind her head, trying hard to remember what had happened before she was brought here. But nothing came to her except a vague sense of a dim place and the sudden sight of Sam. She sidled down the bed and drifted back into an uneasy sleep. Once again she was inside the hidden half of her life, the secret place that spellbound and overshadowed her. Nimbus was running through Bones Wood, calling her name, leading her on and on. She was following, tripping up, trying to catch him up, so that when she opened her eyes and saw him at the window, softly calling her, she thought it was part of her dream. He pointed impatiently to the window catch but she turned away. When she looked back he was up on the windowsill, his hand pushing through the top opening, probing the latch of the larger window below.

Chloe froze. A crack in her imagination took her to the dark stone tunnel. Panicking, she leapt out of bed and ran downstairs to the front door. Desperately, she tugged at it but Leela had double locked it. She ran into the kitchen – and stopped, seeing through the window the bottom rungs of the ladder Nimbus had pushed against the wall. The metal struts were like a cage. She remembered how she had once trusted him. What had happened to make her so afraid?

She went back upstairs to her bedroom and found him opening the window, leaping lightly into the room. He stood absolutely still, his eyes on hers. 'I want you to follow me, Chloe. You're one of our tribe. We want you to be with us.'

With a flash of insight into how she had once felt, Chloe said, 'I've changed.'

Nimbus pulled her roughly towards him. 'Nothing can make you change,' he said.

There was something in his voice, something so compelling, that she almost lost herself again. She managed to ease herself away from him. 'I'm staying here.'

She pushed at Nimbus but he had the anchor cross in his hands. He twisted it, pulling it tightly round the front of her neck. She couldn't breathe, she couldn't see, and then the chain snapped and she fell crying to the floor. He stood over her, staring down.

'Looking for you all night,' he said, as if he could read her thoughts. With the palms of his hands towards her he made round movements in the air. He swayed his arms from side to side as if he was orchestrating her feelings, drawing her back and back to the other world where she once belonged. His voice was deep, hoarse. 'We haven't long. You'll follow me now, Chloe. We'll go up the hill together. From now on you'll only listen to me.'

His voice had become slow and hypnotic. He began to count from ten down and each number fell like a bell on her ears. Chloe tried to replace the hypnotic numbers with the sound of church bells. She pictured a great bell going up and down, up and down, and when the numbers grew more insistent she made the church bells ring louder.

Nimbus tied her arm to his with a thin leather belt and forced her out of the bedroom and down to the kitchen. He unlatched a window and pulled her through. In the open air, Chloe's strength was reinforced by the flowers that held her in a ring of colour and perfume. In a flash she saw her mother, her father, Sam, the old house, her old school friends, Aidan, Leela, all of them holding hands to protect her. She felt a sense of sharp regret as Nimbus trampled over the garden, pulling her roughly over the crushed plants.

'I don't need to be tied to you, Nimbus,' she said in a soft, wheedling voice. 'My arm's hurting and we'll go more quickly side by side.'

'Time,' said Nimbus grimly. 'You'll soon forget the meaning of time.'

'We'll run up the hill together,' said Chloe, putting on a dazed voice. Nimbus seemed to believe her and he started to undo the leather belt, pulling at her arm as if she had no feeling. He loosened the knot and she thought: I must wait for the right moment. As if on a whim, he folded the belt and held it in his hand.

They entered the wood and followed the trail to the Nimbus Tree. Reaching it, Nimbus stopped and Chloe sank to the ground as if to recover her strength. He put his fingers on the gnarled trunk and followed the letters he had carved:

ROSIE NEVER FORGOTTEN

Nimbus looked hard at Chloe. "There's not a mark on this tree that don't remind me of my Rosie. And you remind me of her too. You'll die – as George Penfold died, to pay the price of my Rosie's death. When they find you dead as this tree that was struck by lightning in the great storm, they'll never again question my strength and power. That is,' he looked at her cunningly, 'unless you tell me more about the map and lead me to the treasure. Like that I'll get out of here a rich man and go away with Tammy who's all that's left me.'

He's mad, thought Chloe fearfully, why didn't I see this before? Her fear gave her strength and she climbed slowly to her feet, nodding vaguely at Nimbus as if she was in a trance. She walked towards him, doing her best to seem weak and ill but when she was close enough, she let fly, kicking his bad leg as hard as she could. Nimbus lost his balance and fell, and Chloe kicked him again. And then she ran away, heart in her mouth, sprinting from bush to bush, stumbling in the undergrowth, hiding behind trees.

She caught a glimpse of him standing at the edge of the pit but she didn't slow down. Trying to keep to the plantation of firs where the ground was soft and silent, she pushed on. When at last she reached the tree that Aidan had cleared, she was unaccountably strengthened. She stopped, breathing raggedly, listening for footsteps, but another sound filled her head. The singing of the psalms rose up from the ancient chapel that had once stood here. Standing there, Chloe thought she heard the muffled beat of galloping, but it was no longer Dark Time, it was the King himself. She experienced all this in a second and then ran on. She heard shouts from the wood and saw the buzzard fly up and away. By now she was prepared to break cover. She raced out of the shelter of the trees and across to the first gate that led to Kingsholt. Down in the valley, she could see the path that wandered towards Leela's cottage. She longed to run back there but she dared not. Instead she climbed the gate and ran up the drive away from Kingsholt. It took her some time to reach the next gate, the one that gave onto the road. Blackburr Fort was almost opposite on the other side and one or two people were climbing the ditches and grassy walls.

Chloe made for the phone box. Her hands were shaking as she dialled 999.

Chapter Fourteen

Just as Aidan was packing his haversack, Leela came in. Sam offered to make her coffee.

'Yes please,' Leela said. 'And I can tell you that all's fine. Chloe has slept and eaten very well. She's almost her old self.'

'It would be cool to see her like that,' said Sam. 'I can't remember the last time.'

Aidan smiled. 'We have very good news too, Leela. Unbelievable news.' He watched her sit down and place her hands round her mug. 'We've found the original map! It was Sam who made it happen – he discovered a puppet box in the attic and inside there was a piece of very old paper, with some strange clues that Emily Penfold had written down. Sam was a real slave driver and made us work them out! We've been up digging all night, or nearly all night.'

'No!'

'Yes, Leela, it's true. Now drink up, and we'll all go out together.' Aidan turned to Sam. 'We'll call in on Chloe briefly before we go up to the wood.'

'She'd very much like that,' said Leela. 'I think she's beginning to miss you all.'

Judy led the way, exploring all the smells in the thickly growing weeds that lined the track. They rounded a bend and took the short grassy path down to the cottage.

'What's happened?' Leela stopped and pointed. 'What's happened to the flowers?'

'Some wild —' began Sam.

'Maybe a fox?' said Tyler.

Leela shook her head in disbelief. 'Marigolds, poppies, heartsease charlock – all trampled into the ground. It's a sacrilege.'

She ran across the garden and put the key in the lock.

'Chloe, Chloe!'

There was no reply. The kitchen and bedroom windows were open and the house was silent.

'The bastard,' shouted Sam. He ran out of the door, up the field and into Bones Wood. Not far ahead he thought he saw a downy white shadow crossing the trees. The vision gave him a moment of comfort but it soon vanished and when the birds flew up, wing to wing, his anger and panic returned. What was that madman doing to Chloe? He reached the Nimbus Tree and touched the dead bark, feeling the word ROSIE beneath his fingers. At last he began to calm down and for a brief moment he even understood the obsession that drove Nimbus to mark a tree with the name of the daughter he loved. Sam drew strength from his understanding. He could fight an enemy he knew.

By the time Aidan and Tyler caught up with him, his harsh breathing had subsided and he felt, behind his sense of emptiness, something else, strengthening him, knitting him back together, something he did not understand. He looked up at Aidan.

'I didn't mean —'

Aidan smiled. 'Those feelings will help you, they'll drive you on.' He swung the haversack onto the ground. 'A change of plan. We'll have to divide up to find Chloe. Leela is staying in the cottage to guard it. One of us will have to explore the valley—'

'I'll go underground,' said Sam without hesitating.

'Me and Judy'll go with you,' said Tyler loyally.

Aidan gave Sam the haversack. 'I know you both hate the dark,' he said appreciatively.

Together they studied the map and when Sam began to shiver Aidan listed the types of stone that made up the valley, as if it would calm him down. 'First there's chalk, then flint, then limestone – hard and yellowish. Then nodular chalk, with little shell fragments, a cockly bed— 'He looked up at Sam. 'It's important to be strong, especially as I can't go down with you.'

'Message received.' Sam packed away the map and Aidan put

his hands on Sam's thin shoulders. 'It's an important mission,' he said slowly.

When they reached the pit they silently parted company.

'Two's better than one,' said Tyler comfortingly.

Sam put his hand up to his nose. 'You're dead right. Especially as this pit stinks worse than ever.'

'Tie something round your face,' said Tyler.

Sam wished he had thought of that before leaving Kingsholt, but he was wearing nothing that would do and had to bear the stench of decay as he slid down the pit behind Tyler. He watched as Tyler struggled with the door, straining at it . But the iron door refused to budge. 'You have a go," said Tyler stepping back. 'I can't open it.'

Sam slid down to the ledge of stones where he had stood before with Chloe, and pulled on it with all his might. As he let go he almost toppled over into the pit below. Tyler tried again but the iron door was still wedged tight.

'It's Nimbus, he's closed it up.'

Sam didn't dare to think what he might find on the other side. 'Let's try it together.' They both heaved at the solid iron. door. Recklessly, Sam threw every ounce of strength into it and suddenly, his feet slipped. Instinctively he clutched at a tree root, halting his plunge downward towards the bones and the stench of evil. Above him Tyler lay stretched out, head down, reaching for him.

'I've got strong arms,' he whispered, 'you can trust me.'

Slowly, inch by inch, he dragged Sam up and up, until they were side by side on the precarious ledge. 'We're never going to open that door,' Sam said bitterly. Together they climbed out of the pit. Sam took the map out of the haversack and studied it. 'Here's the other anchor cross,' he said, showing Tyler. 'It's where your cottage stands. There might be another entrance.'

'The cellar,' said Tyler. 'Mum always said there were rumours.'

'We have to try everything,' Sam urged. 'Come on, Tyler, back to yours. There might be another way!'

As they ran through the wood, sunlight dropped down on them like a white bird.

Sam and Tyler tore at the wallpaper that covered the door leading down to the cellar. Leela helped them and soon they were standing in a pile of ragged strips.

They heaved against the cellar door but it wouldn't budge. Sam looked at Leela. 'Is there anywhere you might have put the key?'

'I told you, I threw it away. I didn't want Tyler to get lost. It was very difficult to keep an eye on him when he was smaller.'

'Is there *anything* we can use?' Sam emptied out his jeans' pocket. 'All useless.' He handed Leela the quill, the old ink bottle, the piece of chalk and the scraper.'

'Keep them,' said Leela. 'You may need them, you never know. And put on the anchor cross. It's my belief you should wear it. And take these.' She took a pair of white cotton gloves out of her pocket.

'You must be joking,' said Sam, but he took them and stuffed them into the haversack. She's more persuasive than my mum, he thought, as he also allowed Leela to pull the cross over his head and stuff the rubbish back into his pocket.

'You must have *something* to open the door,' he said in desperation.

After a frantic search, Tyler found an old iron hook and wedged it into the large keyhole. It seemed forever before the lock eased back and he and Sam pitched themselves at the door.

At last it groaned open. They flashed their torches down a narrow stone stairway that led to the cellar. It was empty and dank, with the smell of rust and mildew. Sam and Tyler went down the steps into another world.

'Good luck!' Leela's voice echoed from above.

Sam felt in his jacket pocket and gave Tyler the piece of chalk. 'If you make arrow marks en route, we'll be able to find our way back.'

Tyler sniffed, peering uneasily into the dark hole at the far end of the cellar. 'I don't like it. There's nothing to hold on to.' He gave Sam a worried look.

'That's why we need the arrow marks.'

At that moment Judy came bounding down the steps.

'I'm not going without her,' said Tyler.

'Then put her on a lead.'

Tyler shook his head. 'She's never been on a lead.'

Sam nodded and they set out with Judy. Quite quickly, the cellar gave way to a man-made tunnel, propped up by ancient timbers. Sam flashed his torch at the walls and highlighted scratched graffiti on the overhead beams. Despite the damp and dark they walked fairly quickly.

'We're going up,' said Tyler edgily. He stopped to make an arrow mark on the wall. Judy turned and waited. Tyler's breath was coming in short, uneven, spasms. 'I don't like it down here, I feel closed in. I don't know the way.'

Sam ignored the panic in Tyler's voice. He had no wish to travel on his own.

A little further on, a corridor branched off to the right. 'Which way do we go?' he asked, hoping, as much as anything, to distract Tyler.

Tyler pointed to the right hand turn. 'I think that leads back to Kingsholt. Straight ahead's the wood. I'm not sure Sam, I just think that's how it is.'

Another intelligence, a different sort. Sam was remembering what Leela had told him. 'I'll take your word for it,' he said.

The sides of the tunnel became rough, pitted with stones and shells and brown stains. They must be going through a different layer of rock, thought Sam – moving up through a million years. They rounded a corner and there it was, the passage where Chloe had been tied up. 'There's the door in the pit,' he said. 'At least Nimbus won't expect us to be down here.'

They squatted against the wall and as Sam took the map out of the haversack, he noticed Tyler's hand was shaking.

'Hey, keep the torch steady,' he said, adding after a few moments, 'There! That's where they built the chapel in the stone mines. On the other side of a great wall.' He carefully put away the map.

'It'll be all right,' he said to Tyler as they set off again.

A little further on the corridor widened abruptly, giving way to a huge, hewn room, an underground hall. As Sam flashed his torch round the six passages that led off from it, Judy disappeared down one of them.

Panic stricken, Tyler watched her go. 'I can't go on without Judy. I've got to get out, Sam!' His shaking torch rippled light on the walls. His breath was coming in short, sharp gasps.

Sam looked into his eyes and saw the panic. 'Can you get back on your own, Tyler?'

'I've got the arrow marks,' said Tyler, 'but I can't leave you and Judy.'

'Don't worry about us. She'll smell her way back to me and I'll be all right with her.' Sam did not know where his courage came from.

'I'll try and track you from above,' Tyler said breathily. 'There's another entrance, isn't there, near the lost chapel, by Blackburr Fort. I found it ages ago. It's by a tree, I think. I'll go up there.'

He turned back gasping for air, even though the temperature was cold and even.

'Look out for the arrow marks,' Sam shouted after him. Then he realised Tyler had the chalk and he wouldn't be able to mark his own way back.

The temptation to run after him was great but somehow he resisted. 'I'll photograph the way in my head,' he decided as he looked at the map, studied it carefully then put it back into the haversack. He had found courage from somewhere but he still needed to hold on to something, so he clutched the scraper in his pocket.

A drifting fell on him, a falling through time. When the dog raced up to him and licked his face it seemed to him that it was not Judy but the saluki dog from Kingsholt. She was alive and sleek, her eyes glistening with warmth, her feathery tail waving.

'The ancient hunter dog,' whispered a voice inside his head. 'She runs across hot sands and holds the gazelle in her soft mouth.'

Sam watched the dog move towards the first tunnel on his left. She looked back at him, eyes shining, then disappeared into the dark. Sam followed. He was no longer afraid. He recalled the workmen who had hacked into the walls from Roman times and he thought he recognised them in the shadow behind the torch-light, chipping and shaping the stone so it fell in oblongs. He saw the half blind horses pulling the heavy trucks full to the brim and the graves of men and boys buried under the fall of stones. He lowered the beam of the torch down onto the damp ground where the dog's light paw marks showed him the way. Suddenly a noise grew out of the darkness, thin, malignant, ricocheting off the rough surfaces, The dog was at his side again, sleek, long-legged, eyes gleaming like glass. She trotted a little in front of him and somehow Sam found the courage to follow as he listened to the groans, high pitched screeches, sobs that fell like black water.

Slowly he felt himself change; he was no longer good old Simon Penfold from Cheriton Street, Balham. He was clothed in someone else's mind, someone older, wiser but who was also at the edge of desperation.

He looked down at himself. Over his leather jacket he seemed to see an insubstantial white robe. He realized the noises he was hearing were the cries of the massacre.

He had no need to look at the map or follow the dog. Hadn't he helped the lay brothers build the chapel and the great arch over the three tunnels?

He whistled for his saluki and together they made their way down the right hand passage.

The path was steep and the roof low. It would not be difficult to block it off from the Viking marauders. He stopped. A tunnel joined the one on which he was travelling, a natural path the river had forged. The Brothers called it Devil's reach, for its darkness bore the stench of a timeless Hell. He heard the pounding of hooves, rhythmic, ringing, coming up the centuries towards him. Out of that darkness he imagined the wild eyes of the black horse, its foaming mouth, its ears sharp and upward, its black skin sleek and sweaty.

Dark Time's sword gleamed in his pale hand. There were only a few paces between Sam and its sharp point. I've nothing to fight with, he thought, no sword, no shield, only a monk's robe to protect me and a monk's dog at my side. Yet I must send him back to the Hell from where he came.

In his new, wise mind, he undid his jacket and lifted up Leela's anchor cross. The dog loosened a sharp pebble from the ground and Sam picked it up and threw it. A soundless scream came out of Dark Time's black open mouth. His horse reared in panic then turned and galloped back into the darkness of Devil's Reach.

Sam stood still, breathing hard, then followed the saluki as she raced ahead and stopped in front of the great wall the lay brothers had made to guard their treasure.

Once again something so strong swept over Sam that he was forced to shut his eyes. It was like a wave of time dragging him back, pulling him down to the floor. After an unknowable length of time it receded, taking with it the sharpness of massacre, the stench of pestilence. He opened his eyes and looked down. He no longer wore the white floating robe, though wisps of the monk's memory still clung to him. The dog was no longer the sleek, swift, shiny-eyed saluki. Instead the dumpy, black form of Judy was beside him, nuzzling his hand, looking up with her warm, friendly, commonplace eyes.

And he was Sam Penfold again, from Cheriton Street, Balham, London. A steady attitude and a good memory, his report had said. He took the map out of his haversack and studied it again. On paper, the wall he sat against was nothing but a small dot and there was no indication of how to get through it. Sam put away the map and flashed his torch over the smooth stone. Finding nothing, he held the torch in his mouth and passed his hands slowly and carefully over every slab. His heart beat fast as he put his thumb against a pebble, encased in the lowest and largest slab of all; his last chance! He pushed, hearing it click against something. Slowly, the huge, hewn stone swivelled round.

'Look at that, Judy.'

With the dog at his heels, Sam crawled through the hole into the darkness beyond. In front of him was a small, simple chapel. He went inside through a rounded, yellow limestone arch and stood in front of a bare altar that was also cut out of the yellowish limestone. Wisps of the monk's memory made everything familiar – the anchor cross above the altar, chiselled simply from the stone, the stations of the cross round the wall, also carved from stone, the bareness. Sam played the torchlight over the altar but it revealed no secret sign. He flashed the beam onto the anchor cross. Was that a pebble in its centre? He touched it with his forefinger and to his surprise it sprang open, revealing a wide gap at the back of the altar. Holding his breath, he pulled out the box the monk had once put there in a hurry because the Vikings had found the entrance to the mines and were almost upon him.

The box was heavy; Sam heaved it onto the altar. It was made of oak and a piece of vellum had been stuck to the lid bearing the words: *We must hide this great book but hope that one day…*

He knew what to do. In the silence he took out his ink and quill and finished the sentence in the same beautiful script. *We must hide this great book but hope that one day it will be found.*

Now he, Sam Penfold of Cheriton Street, Balham, was one of the long line of scribes who had cared for the great volume inside the oak box. He couldn't resist prising open the gold clasp.

He was not disappointed. Inside was a magnificent book, beautifully bound in tooled leather. He carefully placed it on the altar beside the oak box and took the cotton gloves out of the haversack. Now he understood.

The pages were made of vellum and covered with beautiful writing. He couldn't understand the Old English but he recognised the words, Psalmus David, in the introduction to the second psalm. A glow of excitement went through him. That was the introduction Aidan had read to him all those days ago. Now he had no doubt that this book was King Alfred's translation of the first fifty psalms. He stood for a long time turning the beautiful, illuminated pages, until he remembered he had to hurry. He closed the great book very carefully then put it back into the oak box. He secured the lid and put the box on the altar while he emptied all the stuff in the haversack into his jeans and leather jacket pockets. Then, with great care, he placed the box into the haversack and put it over his shoulders. He left the ink and the quill on the stone altar as a sort of offering, and took a last look round. Almost regretfully, he squeezed through the low slab, pressed the pebble and watched the stone swing back.

Only a minute or two had passed when he heard the scream. *'I'm coming after you, wherever you are.'*

It was Nimbus, and he was after him. Or was he looking for Chloe? Sam ran quickly down the tunnel with his heart in his mouth. He was no longer able to navigate and followed Judy into a narrow crevice in the right hand wall of the tunnel, thinking, hoping, there might be a quicker way out. They were moving up, higher and higher and Sam felt quite jubilant until he looked ahead and saw a huge boulder obstructing the tunnel.

A sense of despair overwhelmed him and when, from

somewhere behind him, he heard horse's hooves thunder through the tunnel, he was sure Dark Time was coming for him. He sat down, panic stricken. Sweating with fear, he felt in his pockets for a tissue. Instinctively he took hold of the scraper and waved it in the air in the forlorn hope that it would rescue him. All this time, Judy was watching him with a blank expression in her eyes.

Suddenly, a deafening noise filled the tunnel. Sam held his head in his hands and hunched up next to Judy. When he had the courage to look up, he saw the boulder had cracked into a V shape. It was a miracle! In his gratitude Sam kissed the scraper. What extraordinary magic powers it had! He put it carefully back into his pocket and hugged Judy who was still shivering with fear.

Sam whistled to her as he led the way through the V shape. He found himself in a man-made tunnel, with wooden planks securing the roof and the sides. As he climbed the rough path, Judy followed, whimpering a little. Sam turned round to comfort and encourage her. With his photographic memory firing on all cylinders he repeated Aidan's words in reverse. *First there's a cockly bed, then nodular chalk with little shell fragments, then limestone, hard and yellowish, then flint, then chalk.*

'I hope you understand,' he said to Judy. He had the impression the dog nodded and he smiled.

They were going up through millions of years and now the walls were packed with flints. At the end of the dark tunnel was a white light, high up, as if it hung in space. It was like a torch, bobbing and circling to convey signals. Judy scampered ahead, running fast when she heard Tyler's voice filling the darkness.

'Is that you, Sam?'

'You can say that again!'

Judy was already prancing ecstatically round Tyler as Sam clambered out of the tunnel. It seemed as if he had been in the dark forever.

It took time to take in sunshine, grass, sky. The word, innocent, came into his head for that is how it seemed, innocent and open and free.

'Blackburr Fort,' said Tyler. 'We're high up here. I found the entrance ages ago, when I was playing gardening. I dug down and found this lid. It was hard to open, and I quickly put it back when I saw the dark tunnel. It was a bit harder to find this time because everything's overgrown.' He patted Judy on the head. 'She's clever, isn't she? I think she's the cleverest dog in the world!'

Chapter Fifteen

Sam and Judy had come up right beside one of the trees that grew in the enclosure of the fort. Once cattle and people had lived here together but now it was a wild grassy stretch, shaded by a few trees, with a little pathway that ran high up along its surrounding bank.

Sam took off his haversack and put it beside him as he lay on his back and looked up. How light the world was! While he was resting, Tyler and Judy went for a circular walk round the fort. To Tyler's surprise he saw Aidan and Chloe coming towards him.

Sam's down there,' shouted Tyler, pointing to his friend. Chloe ran down the slope and across the grass.

'Hi!' she shouted. 'You're safe and sound, that's all that matters.'

Sam sat up and grabbed hold of his haversack. 'Not all,' he said and his eyes sparkled.

'Do you mean you've —'

Sam nodded. 'I'll tell you everything later,' he said, as if talking about the book might put it in danger. Chloe looked at him with new respect. 'A knight in shining armour!'

They all walked back together. Halfway down the drive, at the bend where Kingsholt came in sight, a police car stopped and an officer rolled down the window. 'Any idea where Nimbus is?' He nodded at Chloe. 'This young lady told us enough for us to want to question him.'

'His cottage is over there, 'said Aidan, pointing to the field at the top of the valley. 'Whether he's there I don't know, but, yes, you must find him as soon as you can. He's a dangerous one.'

The officer nodded. 'We'll have a look round.'

When the noise of the police car had faded from the valley, Aidan led the way back to Kingsholt.

That evening, after supper, they all sat round the cleared

table. Sam put the box ceremoniously onto a white cloth that Aidan had found. With a sense of triumph he put on Leela's white gloves and brought out the book.

They sat in silence round him, awed by the old writing and the illuminations that were all done by hand.

'It *is* the psalms translated by King Alfred,' said Aidan in a voice that betrayed his joy. 'The script is an English variant of the Carolingian miniscule.' Forgetting, in his excitement, that Sam was the only one who had any interest in the names of scripts he went on in a hushed voice, 'I should think it was copied in the tenth century, a hundred years after King Alfred translated the psalms into his own language. Early English,' he added and then he was silent as he put on Leela's gloves and turned the pages for himself.

'Tomorrow I'll take it up to the British Library,' said Aidan, 'and see what they have to say.'

'And we'll go swimming,' said Sam. 'Won't we, Chloe?'

'I'm really tired,' she said, 'but it might be an idea to do something normal. I haven't used my cozzie for ages.'

That night Chloe and Sam slept peacefully at Kingsholt. At last the shadow of the past had moved away, like a cloud from the sky, and left their minds free and clear. They had no dreams, no nightmares, only a long refreshing sleep. Outside the summer stars shone clearly and the moon hung gold above the valley until it faded into the light of dawn.

It was two days before Aidan came back from London. 'The curator was amazed,' he said to Sam and Chloe. 'He told me the book is invaluable and they hope to raise enough money to buy it. Of course, we'll share whatever we get but this means I can fulfil George's dreams. How can I thank you all enough?'

'And the police have found Nimbus,' said Chloe. 'It was on the local radio and Leela brought in this newspaper. Here it is:

The police found a man who called himself Nimbus clambering up from a pit on the Kingsholt estate. They took him and his daughter in for questioning. His daughter has gone to live with her mother and Nimbus is in custody awaiting trial.'

'What a relief for us all,' said Aidan.

Several days later, everyone was once again seated round the kitchen table but this time listening to Dorothy Penfold, who had rushed back when Aidan at last contacted her. She looked anxious and serious, an emotion that didn't quite suit her laid-back appearance. 'Jack and I have been talking,' she said, a little quicker than usual. 'We've come up with some ideas and we'd like to put them to you before Sam goes.' She smiled at him gratefully. 'The long and the short of it is, we think we've made a mistake imagining we could live here. Especially when I consider,' she faltered and bit her lip, 'all that's happened.' She looked at Chloe. 'You're on the mend, darling, but I should have been around and I should have understood more. Anyway, Dad and I think we should go back to our old house and let Aidan develop this one. We *will* be part of it but it's better if we don't live here.' She held out her hand to Chloe. 'Then you can go to your old school and have fun again.'

Chloe leaned forward and took her mother's hand. 'Do you mean it, Mum?'

Mrs Penfold gave her a small smile. 'Yes, I do. After all we haven't sold the old house and Dad'll still be able to help Aidan carry out his plans. So you can come here, but not live here. What do you think?'

Chloe wandered over to the window. The valley was peaceful now, and she was enjoying it for the first time in many months. But she thought with longing of her old house, her old school, her old friends. She turned round slowly. 'If we did go back, we'd have the best of both worlds. What do you think, Sam?'

He grinned. 'I'm all for having my cake and eating it.'

Dorothy Penfold turned to Aidan. 'And what about you, Aidan?'

His grey eyes looked thoughtful and a little sad. 'Of course, I'll miss you all but —' He looked at Chloe. 'I'd like you to lead a normal life, with ordinary friends.'

'That's what we feel, darling,' said her mother. She looked up at the cobwebs no one could reach. 'It's all been too much for me as well. I can see that now. I think that's why I kept going away.'

'I'll come and cook for you,' said Sam to Aidan, 'and when the place is set up, I'll be the chef.' He felt as if he wanted to go on being a part of the valley. He wasn't sure how it would work out but it seemed like the right direction.

'That's nice,' said Dorothy, 'and maybe your mother could come down for a visit.'

'Mum's a law unto herself,' said Sam. 'When I phoned her and hinted at what had happened, all she said was, I sounded different and was I any taller?'

They all laughed and Sam went over to the Aga. 'Chef's special,' he said, bringing out a huge, bubbling lasagne.

The day before Sam went home, he went for a walk with Chloe and Tyler, right round the valley. They started out from Kingsholt and followed the footpaths that circled the estate, through the wild woods and the neglected fields. When they drew near to the pit they lapsed into silence. But they had nothing to fear for Aidan had already begun to fill the dark hole with the branches he had cut down. There was no stench now, no sense of horror. Light played through the trees where he had been working and a huge stone marked the place where the chapel would be. It was like an act of faith.

The path led to a hidden field where young foxes were playing in the grass. Tyler insisted on watching for some time and as Sam persuaded him to move on, a stray deer crossed their path, eyeing them shyly. 'Do you remember Bambi?' said Chloe, as the animal bound away. 'We saw it one summer when we were really small.' She still felt fragile and unsteady but all the bad memories were already losing their power. They chatted and laughed as they walked and when they finally skirted the hill behind Kingsholt they stopped and looked down at the crumbling mansion.

'It somehow looks better already,' said Sam. 'It must be seeing it from a long way off.'

'It feels different,' said Chloe, 'as if someone good has woken up and done away with all the darkness.' She sat down on the grass. 'I've been feeling so strange,' she said, half to herself, 'but now I wonder if there was a purpose behind it all.'

Sam sat beside her. 'If it hadn't happened, we'd never have found the book and you would never be going back to your old school and friends.'

Tyler chewed a piece of grass. 'I wish you were staying.'

Sam punched him. 'Don't be daft. We'll come back.' He paused. 'Things move on. I wonder if we'll ever hear the singing again.'

'That sort of thing never happens twice,' said Chloe.

'If Aidan builds the chapel, somebody will sing in it,' said Tyler.

'*You would* have the right answer,' said Sam as they scrambled down to Kingsholt.

'Look,' said Tyler, half-way down the hill. 'There's the buzzard. Up there. It'll soon be migrating.'

Sam and Chloe shielded their eyes against the sunlight. They caught their last glimpse of the great bird as he rose from the trees, circled round and flew away.

OUR STREET
BOOKS

Our Street Books for children of all ages, deliver a potent mix of
fantastic, rip-roaring adventure and fantasy stories to excite the
imagination; spiritual fiction to help the mind and the heart
grow; humorous stories to make the funny bone grow; historical
tales to evolve interest; and all manner of subjects that stretch
imagination, grab attention, inform, inspire and keep the pages
turning. Our subjects include Non-fiction and Fiction, Fantasy
and Science Fiction, Religious, Spiritual, Historical, Adventure,
Social Issues, Humour, Folk Tales and more.